THE GLASS MASK

Monsters Lurk Beneath

E.L. DuBois

FOR SKYLAR

~ * ~

To all those who have endured, may you never
be silenced.

ACKNOWLEDGEMENTS

Thank you to my amazing husband, beautiful daughter, and wonderful parents. Without your love and support, this would not have been possible. Thank you for never giving up on this lost soul.

To my little brother, the true writer, and my first partner in crime. I love you. You have been there encouraging me from the very beginning. I will always believe in your dreams and be your number one fan. Never give up. Your talent is a gift to this world.

AUTHOR'S NOTE

Sins, sins, sins
she says with a grin
Vanity, adultery, lust, and greed
Lies, beautiful lies are all she may need
A fast track to Hell on path of her making
It will take every ounce of will to survive without
breaking

By society's standards, I have sinned more than my fair share. But has my suffering and penance been enough to redeem myself? If there is indeed something more beyond this life, where will I end up? These are the thoughts that resonate through my mind. Morbid thoughts, thoughts laced with an anxiety that ways upon my chest. Thoughts that should not be plaguing me anymore... but they do. As I sit at the second-hand, round, antique wooden table, snuggled in a corner of the modest home where I find solace, my mind retreats to darker times. It is during mornings like this, when the house is quiet, that

I cannot stop my thoughts from drifting to the path I have taken.

My hands are wrapped tightly around my favorite coffee mug. The one that says, *Worlds Greatest Mom* in bold, pink lettering. The briefest of smiles play across the naturally turned down corners of my lips, as I fondly remember the day my truest joy gave me the cup. I watch as the creamy, latte-colored liquid swirls and goes cold.

My thoughts turn even darker to the days before and after my truest joy came into my life. A sigh escapes my lips as I run one finger around the rim, down the side of the cup, bringing it to rest along the wood grain of the table. I know that like me, this table has seen too much. Felt too much. Survived too much.

I am only thirty-seven, that is nothing in age... but I feel seventy-three as I think about the past ten years of my life. I am so tired, more tired than I should be for my age. A bone-deep tiredness resonates to my very soul.

The kind of tired that makes a person want to give up.

The kind of tired that makes me doubt the happiness I now have and worry of losing every day... because I'm not worthy.

The kind of tired rooted in despair and insecurity.

The kind of tired only the truly broken would understand.

The kind that makes a person want to crawl into a hole somewhere – curl into a ball and disappear forever.

I cannot, however, give in to this tiredness.

I have a family that depends on me. Loved ones that need my strength and support.

So... I carry on. Always ready to cater to the ones that need me. Care for the sick, be the strength, and smile always, even when it feels like I'm dying inside.

Smile always. That is the motto of this sinner.

When I think of the person I was, it's like I am telling someone else's story. Confessing someone else's sins.

The most common and belittling questions a person can be asked when it becomes known that they were a victim of domestic abuse is:

"Why didn't you just leave?"

"How could you stay?"

or "Why didn't you say something?"

The answer, much like life, is both simple and complex.

Simple version: "Because I couldn't leave,

nor could I go. And the silence... it was and still is, deafening." The complex version is one even I myself don't understand.

I live with the guilt every day, that my silence and inability to speak out has allowed a monster to walk freely among us. That is a heavy burden to bear, one that I will never be able to escape. What exactly do I say to the next victim? "Oh, so sorry I was a coward and kept quiet. I hope my apology heals all the damage he has done."

I know I am not responsible for his actions, but the guilt, damn it, can be all-consuming. Most days, I walk around feeling like I opened Pandora's Box. Satan slithered out and after the proverbial, "Oh Shit!" I was like, "My Bad," right before I ran for the hills, praying no one noticed it was I who had unleashed the beast.

Seriously, folks, I am that dramatic, and this is how I feel. My cowardice could cost someone else their life. This is the shit that plagues me. FYI, I didn't always have a foul mouth. One acquires these traits in dire situations. So... I earned it.

Also, I have the attention span of a squirrel. Again, I was not always this way, but I am going to assume it is due to actual brain damage.

With that said, back to the topic. Complex

answer... right. I don't have a definite one. All I have is personal insight to years of abuse, and a will to survive. Which I managed to do, just barely.

I am trying to understand it all, and honestly, maybe my brain will never make sense of it, but part of the conclusion I am coming to is this: to understand where I ended up, one must first get a glimpse of who I was, and the sins I had committed. Now, I am not an overly religious person. I do not sway toward one religion or another. I do pray, I do thank God whoever he/she/it may be, and I do hope that there is something great beyond this life. But, I do believe in Karma. I believe that if you do bad things to hurt someone, the universe will repay you, sometimes tenfold, one way or the other.

So, at some point in my life, I let my believed sins against others fester at the heart of who I was. I demonized myself to the point that by the time I realized I was in the midst of a full-blown living hell, I rationalized it by believing that I somehow deserved everything that was done to me. Because let's face it…Karma is a nasty bitch.

On a very important note, I know now that I deserved none of it. My rationalizations were the desperate attempts of a barely sane woman just trying to survive. No one deserves what I went through, well... almost no one. I am really banking on this Karma thing, because it has a lot of catching up to do with my Monster.

Bitterness, oh thine is my middle name.

It should also be noted that no real names had been used in my story. This is of course to protect certain people from the vile monster that lives behind his glass mask, who has yet to pay for the sins he has committed.

Are you listening, Karma?

It was Hell. Let me reiterate… a living Hell. Nothing was sure then, except fear. Life was uncertain, death always loomed, and instability was the norm.

I believe I became the embodiment of the Mad Hatter. I was once Beauty. She was me. I was her. But she died somewhere along the way, and I took her place. Madness breeds madness and some traumas not even a heroine can come back from. Sometimes, one becomes so broken that the only course of action is the death of one's former self.

Beauty's life spawned the creature I have become today. I crawled from the bowels of darkness created by the unforgivable acts of a monstrous Beast. I will never again be the Beauty I once was, but I can take the pieces of her and mold them into a stronger, more beautiful version. That is who I am becoming.

So, here is my tale of woe. All about how Beauty met the Beast, and how he broke her and murdered her soul. He delighted in remolding her into a truly mad hatter... but she prevailed.

Beauty may have died, but the creature that arose from the ashes in her image is a heroine.

You might find this a truly horrific fairytale, indeed.

No worries... there is a happy ending. Even if the Beast still lives.

ONCE UPON A TIME

Pride, greed, envy, vanity

T en years ago, Beauty had been a stunning, twenty-seven-year-old, ex-beauty
queen, with long raven hair, bold hazel
eyes that twinkled mischievously, and a natural
sweetness that attracted the opposite sex like
bees to honey. So, why wouldn't she believe
that the world was at her fingertips? Shouldn't
she be handed everything she desired effort-
lessly? She was an over achiever with no fear,
no regrets, and the idiotic idealism that she
could do anything... have anything... be whatever she wanted. And why wouldn't she feel
that way? She was exceptionally smart and ex-

celled at everything she tried.

By twenty-three she had a husband that adored her, a great job where she was well-liked and constantly praised. She had even built and owned a beautiful home in a middle-to-upper class subdivision; a part of the affluent community she had grown up in.

In her spare time, she furthered her education and expressed herself through art. She and her husband had decided they didn't want children. They just wanted to focus on themselves, their dogs, and their careers. She had the perfect little life and considered herself luckier than any of the "friends" she had graduated with.

Her husband took care of everything. She had all the comforts a woman would wish for, but instead of appreciating his efforts to shield her from monetary stress, she resented him and felt like he treated her like a child.

She had no idea that she was basically a spoiled brat, an absolute idiot, and a completely deluded, self-proclaimed princess that had a very long fall from grace awaiting her in the near future.

Her perfectly constructed fairy-tale would be no happily ever after at all. She was the dim-witted unsuspecting victim in a real-life horror story. She was that moron girl that runs back into the house when she should be running for help.

Essentially, she was a stunningly wrapped hot mess. A screw-up that would turn everything she touched into crap and hurt anyone who loved her. What no one around her knew was that to her, perception was everything and her "perfect life" was really all a sham. Starting with herself and the mask she wore.

She was insecure, had body image issues, spent years with an eating disorder bouncing between diet pills and bulimia. She had always had this niggling little voice in the back of her mind that said, "You will never be good enough, never be thin enough, pretty enough, smart enough, talented enough," and that voice filled her with self-loathing. A feeling so destructive she would deliberately sabotage all that was good in her life.

When she met her husband, she played games with him. Treating him like a king one minute, then pushing him away just to see if he would go and stay gone. But he never did. He always stayed. He truly loved her, and it secretly ate away at her because she felt undeserving.

Eventually, he asked her to marry him and she said yes. Even though she was too materialistic and screwed up to love him back. She would not allow herself to love her husband the way he deserved to be love. Even going as far as to convince herself she wasn't even attracted to him. She was the pretty one, and he was lucky to have snagged her. She had this idealistic notion of the perfect man, created at a very young age. He would love her unconditionally, be tall, have blue eyes, dark hair and a well-built physique. Most importantly though, because of a strange obsession she had with all things French, he had to be of French descent. It was absurd, but it was the husband she wanted.

Her husband wasn't unattractive. He was of average height, had blonde hair, blue eyes, Irish and a little husky. Physically far from her ideal man. She would tell herself that when they were ninety-eight years old, it wouldn't matter what they looked like because they would both be ugly. She was stupid and focused on his outside appearance, she never noticed that inside, the man she had married was more beautiful than her outward appearance would ever be. He had loved her unconditionally and in return... she broke his heart.

She was so vain that she loved to walk into a room, scan it slyly and know she was the most beautiful girl in it. She loved knowing that when she was on her husband's arm, he was considered the "him" in the phrase "why is she with him?" She was narcissistic and had this preconceived notion that in every relationship there is a power dynamic that goes like this: the more attractive partner has control. This person must always be with someone who loves them more. If the relationship fails, you cannot suffer from a broken heart.

In her mind, she had settled, because she knew her husband loved her more and that brought her moderate comfort. But eventually, that would not be enough.

After her first adolescent heartbreak, which in the bigger scheme of things was nothing, she concluded that she would never give herself completely to anyone again. No one would have the power to break her heart.

At the time, she thought that heartbroken was the only kind of broken a person could become. She had been a fool.

So, at twenty-six, perched upon her self-built monument, she decided to commit sins to sabotage her kingdom. Creating a snowball effect in her life which would teach her to learn the true meaning of *broken*.

* * *

Lust and Adultery

That is right, the beautiful southern princess with the great job, exquisite home, adoring husband and simple drama-free life committed adultery. She didn't just cheat... she went overboard, because you know, if she was going to do something she was going to do it big.

Not too long after turning the twenty-six, she met a person online who lived nine hours away, was five years younger, and again, not her ideal man. He was simply an escape from her life. In a bold move, she uprooted herself; left her husband, disappointed her family, and walked away from it all.

The house, the husband, the job, the life.

The niggling voice at the back of her mind congratulated her for ruining what she felt she had never deserved. However, selfish as she was, she had strung her husband along until she could no longer. Maybe, deep inside, she held out a small hope that she could still get it all back. Maybe, she strung him along out of fear, or simply because she was a coward who could not bring herself to end it.

Either way, she treated the man who loved her like a puppet with strings, to be pulled in the direction she wanted him to go, all the while living with and having a relationship with another man. This lasted for a year and a half.

Having a boyfriend and a husband was hard work, especially when she began to realize that the relationship with the boyfriend was a nightmare. He was immature, selfish and basically a child looking for someone to take care of him. Karma was rearing its ugly head, and she had now taken on the role her husband had with her. She was the caretaker, bearing the financial burden, emotional stress, and responsibility for a selfish person that was never pleased.

Toward the end of the relationship, the unthinkable happened. A routine pap smear showed that she had "abnormal cells." A biopsy showed she had stage two cervical cancer. When she asked the doctor who gave her the news, the doctor responded with, "I'll pray for you." She was devastated. The boyfriend acted as if he didn't care. That was the final nail in the coffin of that relationship.

When she told her husband, he responded with, "I want a divorce."

Feeling alone, not knowing if she would live another six months, she finally felt she had gotten what she deserved. Karma, the nasty bitch, was rearing her ugly head. Pretty little princess had no idea there were fates worse than the dreaded C-word.

After two hopeless weeks waiting to see an Oncologist, she was finally given hope. The Oncologist said she would do everything to ensure that she survived. It was like she had been granted a second chance to be a better person. So, she went through the cancer surgery, followed the doctors' orders, and during this trying time, along came the boy named after a famous outlaw. He would give her the greatest gift and joy of her life but take everything else from her.

1

Lust, diligence, patience, kindness, humility

At twenty-seven years old, and at a very vulnerable time in her life, she met a boy. Not a man, but a boy eight years her junior and a master manipulator. He had an enigmatic smile, blonde hair, clear blue eyes, and at first, said all the things she wanted to hear. He still was not the ideal man she had dreamed of, but he was young, wild, and was only supposed to be a fling.

There was something about his possessive nature that she had tried to understand and was undeniably drawn to. She had never been around someone who wanted to possess her completely, and it stoked her ego. At first, it had been enticing, a little dangerous, and fun. She was enjoying the freedom; going out and having the good times she had missed out on since she had married and settled down so young. The boy had been fond of telling her she was beautiful, smart, funny, and too good for him. All the things she needed to hear to quail the niggling voice at the back of her mind. She became caught up in the whirlwind of lust and romance. She had never met anyone like him.

The intensity of his affections was intoxicating. Within a week, he had told her he loved her, and she had said it back. He had been there for her through the cancer scare, even attending her final doctor's visit. He called and texted constantly. The attention was flattering and overwhelming, and she reveled in it. He acted as if he could not live without her. She was like a life blood to him. Everything he had ever wanted or needed; the very breath in his lungs. So, of course, they could not be apart.

She fell deeper under the spell of their passionate summer romance.

When he suggested they move in together after a month, she hesitated but finally agreed.

There was just something about him that she could not put her finger on. All she knew was that he was impossible to say no to. She should have seen the signs; but she was oblivious. She thought his jealous tendencies were flattering. No man had ever been so attentive and interested in her every action. He had made her believe she was his world and he revolved around her. He made her trust him like she had never trusted before, so she opened up to him about her insecurities, hopes, dreams, and most intimate thoughts. He even managed to make her believe she had broken her rule about loving someone more. She thought, "What else could this be but true love? I have never felt like this before."

Two months into the relationship and she was so enthralled with the intense handsome boy that she missed the subtle changes. She missed the programming. She missed the total loss of herself. She was no longer her own. She was his.

When the backhanded compliments, meant to eat away at her insecurities and not genuine compliments started, she didn't understand that he was mentally breaking her down. He would say things like, "You are so beautiful,"

11

and in the next breath, "You know you are the biggest girl I have ever been with." She wasn't big, but suddenly she was on a diet because she felt huge. He would comment on her age and she developed a new insecurity. Every kindness he gave was followed by a cutting sentiment. He hated that she made more money than him, but had no problems spending it. He would talk about the future and how one day she would not have to work, and he would support them and their children. She had never thought of a life where she didn't work or had kids, but somehow, he made the idea of being a stay at home mommy seem like her dream all along.

By month three, when he had an angry outburst at a family function, she had been sympathetic to his situation. After all, he was the victim of the fight. Someone else had started it and pushed the wrong buttons. It was completely unprovoked, and her poor baby had not deserved to be treated that way. She missed how he methodically consumed every part of her time, until she was cut off from everyone she truly loved. She was from a very close, small family. They were her constant, and her home. Her Mother, the strong and beautiful Queen, was the kind of woman she wanted to be, and her best friend. Her Father, the King, was her protector and the smartest man she knew. She was Daddy's little Princess and she knew he would always be there to save her. Her little brother was her perfect little Prince. They were 10 years apart in age, so he held a special place in her heart. She felt a sister's love, a motherly love, and a special bond with him that was a mixture of kindred spirit and partner-in-crime. They were her Camelot.

Until one day, she looked up and was surprised that they were all out of reach.

The remnants of her home were just hazy images on the horizon. Still there but separated by an indissoluble distance. She had allowed him to cause that wedge, without even realizing he was orchestrating her isolation... until it was too late.

By month five, she was growing weary. The summer was coming to an end and the intensity was overwhelming her. She was contemplating ending the relationship when the unimaginable happened. It was a miracle, but never in a million years did she believe it would happen to her. She found out she was pregnant. More accurately, she took a pregnancy test at home, as a precaution. Being only months away from the cancer scare and on regular birth control, she was not worried. She thought that with every-thing that had happened— the cancer, dieting, the stress — her body was simply telling her to slow down. Then, the test showed two pink lines.

Wait... what? Was all she could process. She kept telling herself, "There must me some mis-take. It must have been a faulty tester." Natu-rally, as any sane Princess in her situation would do, she took five more at-home tests. When they all showed positive results, she called the Queen and freaked out. She insisted that her mother come to her house right away... that all the testers were broken. The Queen calmly told her daughter to get a blood test, and she did. It was positive as well. She was approx-imately six weeks pregnant and in shock.

The Queen, being the true Southern woman that she was, gave her daughter two very im-portant sentiments of wisdom that day. She said, "If you have a baby, you can't be the baby anymore." Then, the gravity of the situation, the pregnancy, her daughter's shock, the fact that she was too young and beautiful to be a Grandma must have set in because she grabbed the Princess and vigorously shook her. "He's 19!

19! You mess around with nineteen-year-olds! You have fun with nineteen-year-olds! You don't get knocked up by one!"

This seemed to bring the Princess out of her stupor.

"The dog ate my birth control. I called the doctor and she said that I was close to my cycle, and to just wait and start my next month's pills after. Then, I called the vet who said the dog would be fine... and he was. He just laid around depressed for a few days, eating everything you put in front of him. I was so worried about the dog I forgot all about my cycle."

This earned the Princess an "I raised you better" look from the Queen.

September 26th, that was the date. It would prove to be one of the best and worst days of her life. The date would be engrained in her memory as one with fleeting hours of joy, followed by the most horrendous cruelty and pain. It was the first time she'd see that her boy was not a boy at all. The boy was the mask of an illusion. What lurked beneath was a Monster far worse than any nightmare. Beauty's frightening Beast was about to emerge.

2

A Slip

She was so confused by the idea of a growing baby. But when the time came to tell the boy about the pregnancy, he was smiling and happy, and she was very surprised. After all, he was only nineteen and had his whole life ahead of him.

When she handed him the paperwork the lab had given her confirming the pregnancy, she told him, "I am a grown woman with my own income. I can do this on my own and will expect nothing from you. You can walk away now and never look back."

He said, "You did this the right way."

She thought that was an odd response and asked, "Right way?"

"Yes, the right way. You confirmed it with the doctor first before telling me. You didn't just pee on a stick and get my hopes up."

She found his behavior odd. *Hopes up?* They had only been in a relationship a few months and he was already hoping for a child? Was he not even going to acknowledge that she had given him a way out?

The boy wanted to celebrate, and like all other things he wanted, he got his way. Beauty's little brother was having a party to celebrate his upcoming birthday, so even though she was tired, she got dressed and they went out.

At the party, the boy had too much to drink and began acting very aggressively toward her brother and his friends. She thought, "It must be the alcohol," and she tried repeatedly to get the boy to come with her and leave. At one point, even gently taking him by the arm and whispering her pleas into his ear. He jerked away and sneered at her. He had never acted in such a way to her before and she was baffled. Maybe he wasn't as ok with the pregnancy as he made her think. Maybe he was freaking out and the alcohol was enabling him to show his true feelings.

As the night progressed, a fight broke out between the boy and her brother. Being the peacekeeper she was, Beauty tried to get the boy into the car and away from the altercation. The boy was enraged; she had never seen anger like that before. He was screaming at her to let him drive. She tried to stay calm, and gently told him that he was in no shape to drive.

She was finally able to get him into the passenger seat and away from the party. As she drove, she could sense that he was still extremely upset. The rage rolled off him in waves, she could almost touch it. The tension filled the car like a palpable entity. She had only made it about a mile down the road, far enough not to be heard or seen by the party goers, when the boy exploded. Screaming at the top of his lungs, he insisted that he wanted to drive.

Shocked and frightened, Beauty still tried to reason with him.

"You can't drive. You've had too much to drink. If our safety isn't important, just think about the babies."

This seemed to placate the boy for the moment. Beauty relaxed as he went silent and she thought all was well. Especially when the boy reached over and lovingly placed his hand in her hair, at the base of her neck. She glanced at the boy to smile, but the smile died on her lips when she saw the answering smile of the thing sitting across from her. Gone was her handsome, sweet boy. In his place was a horrific monster and her blood ran cold. There was such evil in his smile.

Before she could react, the monster gripped her hair and jerked the keys from the ignition with the other. He then proceeded to slam Beauty's face on the stirring wheel several times. The world became hazy as her vision blurred. She could hear a distinct ringing, so loud that she didn't register any of the monster's movements until he opened the driver's door, and wrapped her long, raven hair around his fist.

Their faces were so close, she could smell the alcohol in his breath. Combined with the sickly, metallic taste in her mouth, her stomach turned in disgust.

His words, whispered low and menacing into her ear, were like ice water running through her veins. "I told you I was going to drive, bitch! As for the baby, it makes you mine for good."

Moving across the car seat, the monster then dragged her from the car by her hair and threw her into the passenger seat. The shock had begun to wear off, and the pain started setting in. Beauty began to cry and react. She didn't scream for help. She made no pleas for him to stop. She knew doing so would be futile. The look in his eyes and the tone in his voice told her all she needed to know. Her fate was sealed.

She had not been a child who believed monsters like him existed, but it only took a glimpse at his face and she knew the boogeyman was real.

And she had just tied herself to him for life.

Beauty didn't remember the car ride home or how long it had taken. She didn't register the pain in her head or heart. She only felt a strange numbness as he took her from the car and pulled her into their home. Nothing registered even when he threw her to the ground. She didn't feel him jerking her pants down and ripping her underwear. She didn't even notice the intrusion into her body as he took her violently. The brutality of his actions or her own blood staining the white carpet were not enough to shock her out of stupor. She registered nothing even when his hands wrapped around her throat. Those hands... the ones she thought would only touch her lovingly. They were squeezing her neck... until her vision began to blur. Still, Beauty didn't acknowledge the danger to her life.

None of this is happening. Any moment now, and I'll wake up.

That was Beauty's last thought before everything went black.

3

The pain and the smell of mildew woke her up, but she refused to open her eyes. Her head hurt so bad and she could taste the blood in her mouth. *Did I bite my tongue?* She felt like she had the flu. *Did I get drunk last night? No, that was impossible.* She couldn't have. She was pregnant, and she wouldn't have done anything that could harm the baby. Beauty struggled to recall, but for the life of her, she could not remember why everything hurt.

She lay there breathing and aching for what felt like hours but was probably only minutes. Her brain tried to process the horrible nightmare she had, and why she was in pain. As the events of the previous day arranged itself from being a jumbled mess of hazy images into clearer memories, Beauty's eyes shot open and she tried to sit up.

Naked, she was on the floor of her living room. A blanket had been haphazardly draped over her bruised body. The room was dark, except for small, shimmering rays of sunlight seeping through the blinds. She tried to take stock of her injuries and noticed the purple and yellow marks scattered around her body like a brand. There was a lot of blood. Her blood.

She gasped, her thoughts reeling. "Oh God, the baby!"

It was then she heard a small noise, like someone clearing his throat. Slowly, she lifted her gaze from the floor and her body, until they settled on the ice blue eyes staring down at her. He was sitting calmly on the couch, dressed for work and looking so strange. His face was hidden in shadows, like a villain from some horror thriller. Only his eyes were visible from the stray ray of sunshine that cast itself perfectly across his face.

Instinctively, she scooted back against the wall and wrapped the blanket tighter around her body. Her protective instincts kicked in, although she still could not piece together what happened exactly. She sensed that she was in terrible danger.

They sat in silence, staring at each other until he slowly went down on his knees and crawled toward her.

Still in the shadows, he stopped an arm's length from her and slightly bowed his head. His strange behavior reminded her of a dog cowering. When he looked up at her and the light illuminated his face, she expected to see the horrific monster. Instead, she saw her boy, looking remorseful and sad. She could see the sadness almost consuming him, but she didn't know what to say or do.

His words were a mere whisper in the silence. "I'm so sorry, baby. I'm so sorry. I don't know what came over me. Nothing like that has ever happened before, and it will never happen again. Please... forgive me. Please... don't leave me. I love you and our baby. We're going to be a family. If you don't forgive me and stay, I will kill myself. I can't live without you." Tears began to roll down his cheeks and she just sat there stunned, saying nothing and just staring. Unable to make sense of it all.

He took this as a sign of her forgiveness and pulled her battered body into his arms.

Beauty made no sound, nor did she return the gesture. She felt nothing really, except for the pain in her body. Inside, she felt numb. Like she was watching all of it happen to someone else.

As he cradled her in the silence, she accepted that nothing would ever be the same. Numbness, silence, and pain became her best friends that day. Some sick part of her own mind started to plant the seeds that she deserved everything she got.

Beauty deserved anything the Beast would do to her, because she was unworthy of anything better.

4

A prison with no bars...

After that night, her life changed completely. She wanted to believe him when he said it won't happen again. She convinced herself that if she just loved him enough, he would love her back. She wanted to believe him his apology had been sincere, but sadly it was all an act. The Beast was an expert at lies and manipulation.

The pregnancy was already high-risk. Beatings and rape only increased the danger. Around 12 weeks along, the doctor told her that since three-fourths of her cervix was gone from the cancer, she was already three centimeters dilated. This complication meant she needed to be on bed rest... and no intercourse.

The Beast went with her to all the doctor's visits. In fact, he went everywhere with Beauty; even standing outside the bathroom door. There were no locked doors in the Beast's home. This was a rule.

At the doctor's visits, he would smile, and charm the doctor, nurses, and staff. Always playing the attentive, loving father-to-be and future husband. His excitement over the future baby was evident for all to see. His mask did not even slip when the doctor told her to stay in bed and abstain from intercourse, looking pointedly at the Beast as he did so. This surprised Beauty and worried her at the same time. *What torture does he have in store for me?* she wondered.

He blamed her for everything that displeased him. She was expected to be his slave in all ways, or face punishment. Beauty made more money than the Beast — which he hated — but also expected her to work to support the household and his drug habit. A habit she was unaware of until he chose to reveal them.

Intercourse was expected, sometimes several times, and the way they had sex had changed. He had dropped the preamble of caring for her pleasure and revealed sadistic tendencies she had no idea existed. Aside from drugs, the Beast was addicted to pornography. He favored brutality, strangulation, rape — any act that would shame her or cause her pain. It was the only way he could find his gratification.

So, even though the Beast had smiled and agreed to all the doctor's precautions, he honored none of them.

Beauty worked forty hours a week on her feet, sometimes more. But she was expected to cook, clean, and wait on him hand and foot. The nights were the worst for her. She would be exhausted, but he expected to play with his toy, her, one way or another. Often, the play included violence. It was violence like Beauty had never experienced or even witnessed. The kind of thing that she could only imagine in nightmares.

The Beast was clever with his abuse. He left no visible marks that could not be covered by clothing. He never touched Beauty's lovely face. Spit in it, yes, screamed at it, squeezed it just hard enough to make a point — but never a mark that people could see. Her face was always left pristine to the world.

He pulled her hair and dragged her by it.

But he never yanked any of it out in a noticeable way. He favored kicking, which was quite painful since he also favored steel-toed boots. He enjoyed strangulation and expected that bruising to be covered. Punching and grabbing was always a go-to for the Beast.

The human body can take hits in many places, and no one would know. In one particularly brutal attack, the Beast repeatedly kicked Beauty in her five-month pregnant stomach. She tried to protect her belly and took the hardest blows to her arms and knees. It took at least six weeks of long sleeve shirts to hide her healing wrists. She tended to all her own wounds.

With each hit, she died a little inside. But the physical abuse was not the worst of her torture. No, the Beast reserved that for the bedroom. He raped her in so many ways and violated every part of her body. He could be creative in that area. When the doctor told him they couldn't have intercourse, he took that as a green light to pay special care to other sexual acts. Her tears and pain only brought on his release and made it more intense. He basked in her pain and fed off it. He used bondage and instruments on her. He even had a strange fetish for her breast milk. Feeding from her like a child after torturing her into a state of numbness. This act was especially grotesque to Beauty. Every vile degradation of her body made her feel less of a person and more the Beast's ultimate possession. She felt like a dead body or doll to him. The pregnancy, for him, was like a go-ahead sign to inflict pain on Beauty in every way possible.

It was a thirty-seven-week boot camp of torture. Her body could only take so much. When Beauty was thirty-four weeks pregnant, the Beast became enraged while they were in the car. Beauty had become so numb to the pain and the world that his screams did not cause concern. It was nothing new. Not even when he leaned toward her. Not even when he opened her door. She only felt fear when he unsnapped her seat belt and sneered at her. She tried to stop him. They were driving slowly on a gravel road, what was he planning to do? These thoughts flitted through her mind a second before he pushed her from the moving vehicle. This was how Beauty learned the hard way that humans do bounce.

As she rolled, she tried to cover her belly. Everything had happened so quickly, and she had not even caught her breath when the sharp, excruciating pain started. Then, there was the blood. She had blood on her. Was it from her injuries or was something wrong with the baby?

Oh God, please let my baby be okay. She prayed with all her heart.

His booted feet came into view. The Beast scooped her up in his arms and took Beauty to the hospital. She was surprised by this, the almost tender way in which he carried her. But that quickly faded when she realized that he had only done it because her injuries were not ones she could fix. People will have to help her.

He charmed the hospital staff and played the distraught, worried man perfectly. He even shed tears. The Beast told the staff that Beauty had fallen off the porch and landed in gravel. The hospital staff never questioned this explanation. The truth would have been hard for anyone to even imagine.

Beauty was so frightened and in so much pain. The doctors gave her medicines that made her tired and she vaguely remembered them saying they would need to send her to a larger hospital, one more equipped to handle her situation. She was so out of it, she did not realize that the hospital meant to life-flight her. When the life-flight crew arrived, all she could say was she got seasick. The Beast did all the talking for her. The crew gave her something for nausea and as she watched the liquid slowly creep up her IV she thought, "This is bad. Really bad. Please Lord, let my little girl be okay."

Beauty woke up once in her magical helicopter ride and told the crew, "OHHHH... LOOK AT ALL THE PRETTY LIGHTS!" The rest was just a blur, until the next morning when she awoke, still pregnant, with the Beast by her side.

Every time someone walked into the room, he squeezed her hand painfully. This was his unspoken cue to keep her mouth shut or else. The doctors explained that she had pre-eclampsia. A disorder that affects a pregnant woman's blood pressure, cause seizures, coma, and even death. It also made her retain fluid, and she blew up like the Blueberry girl from *Charlie and the Chocolate Factory* — fifty pounds in three days. This condition can be caused by stress. Naturally, the Beast blamed her work and family to deflect from his own actions. This condition meant Beauty needed to be off her feet and in the hospital, to safeguard the baby's development before birth. The Beast used this as an excuse to be by her side at the expense of his job. Beauty suffered with this condition for three weeks. In that time, the Beast would leave Beauty only when his wicked mother or another family member arrived to watch her. She thought it odd when she senses his eagerness to leave, but secretly cherished the time he was gone.

She would find out years later that every day, he had gone to his father's house and had slept with an old girlfriend who had no clue about Beauty.

Every day, the nurses would come in and say, "No baby today." On the day Beauty turned thirty-seven weeks pregnant, they came in and still said, "No baby today." But when Beauty tried to make a simple trip to the bathroom, her blood pressure spiked. She felt dizzy, and the nurses rushed in. Yes, there would be a baby that day.

The Beast was ecstatic.

Beauty was terrified.

The Beast spent all day calling family members and his friends, rallying them all to the hospital for the birth of his child. With each passing hour, Beauty's terror increased. She was frightened for the birth. Frightened for her child, and worried about how the birth of the baby would change the dynamics of their situation. She prayed that if her love was not enough, maybe the baby's would be. She prayed he would take one look at the little Princess's angelic face and think, "How could I ever continue to hurt the mother of this angel?" Beauty prayed the baby would change everything.

The baby had never turned in Beauty's belly. That, combined with Beauty's condition meant an emergency C-section was the only option for birth. Beauty wanted the Queen by her side. She wanted to hold her mother's hand and feel her comfort in the face of her fear. But the Beast would not allow this. The Queen was devastated, as was Beauty. She hated to see the Beast hurting her mother, but she was paralyzed to do anything. The Beast's word had somehow become law. He would be the only one at Beauty's side during the fear, and he barely contained the glee on his face.

All around them, people believed he was brimming with joy for the birth of his daughter. In reality, he was most excited to see Beauty cut open, and her insides removed. He whispered this fact into her ear as the doctors wheeled her into an operating room. She did not know they would remove her intestines and place them on her chest, and the Beast delighted in informing her of this fact. With each cut, tug, and pull, Beauty could imagine the delight in the Beast's face. The blood and guts excited him.

In that moment, as she watched his Beastly visage flicker beneath his gleeful mask, another piece of her died. He was taking everything from her. Every joy or happiness she had ever felt. The Beast was drawing it out of her soul with each cruel intention and act. Even on the one day in her life that should be most joyous.

With a final yank and release of pressure, the tiny Princess came into the cruel and wicked world of the Beast. She was a tiny beacon of light for Beauty, sparking life back into Beauty's soul. The Beast insisted on being the first to hold the Princess, and as Beauty looked upon the pair, she hoped to see love and light in the Beast's eyes. She thought for a split second that something did flicker across his face. But it was not a father's love. He was proud of his new possession. The ultimate possession because he had created it. The princess was not a person to the Beast. She was a tool. One more weapon of manipulation against Beauty.

When the Beast finally handed the Princess to her and she held her tiny daughter in her arms, Beauty cried with joy. The first true joy she had ever felt in a long time. The little girl was the tinniest, most beautiful being Beauty had ever seen. She felt a love like no other and her heart filled with an instinct to protect and shield the Princess from the Monster lurking over them.

Beauty met the Beast's eyes with a defiance she would never have dared before. In his cold gaze, she saw no love for her or the child. Beauty saw only jealousy for the love she had for the Princess. She saw calculation and a simmering hatred.

Beauty knew several facts at that moment: None of her prayers had been answered. There would be no changing the Beast. No amount of praying or love could turn a Monster into a man. Beauty was going to fight and escape the Beast. Because the most beautiful little Princess in the world had just given her back the will to live.

5

There is no Camelot...

Something had changed in Beauty. Something had re-ignited and the Beast could sense it. From the moment they brought the little Princess home, the Beast began to adjust the manipulation tactics he used on Beauty. He tried to throw her off by acting kind. He was attentive to her and the baby. Old manipulations were back in place, but better this time. He tried to make his possessive nature feel like love.

Even after four days after the Princess's birth, Beauty still had very few memories of the time in the hospital. However, one memory was vivid. The Beast never let her or the Princess out of his sight. He even slept in the hospital bed with Beauty, placing the Princess between them. This went against all instructions by the medical personnel, but the Beast listened to no one. He lived to defy authority.

He tried to persuade her that he was indeed changing because of the baby. She was not fooled. A transformation had happened inside when she had held her child. It was like the Princess was the key to unlocking that awful, charming mask, and the protective instincts that had lain dormant for a long time. Beauty only saw the Beast now and she began to predict his manipulations before he made them. Her life became a dangerous chess game.

Each move he made, she countered. Her actions began to throw the Beast. It took three weeks before he forced himself on her sexually, but Beauty had been anticipating this action. She knew he would never wait for her to heal as the doctor instructed. So, when the time came, and he forced her to do his bidding, instead of crying in pain or lying there numb, she responded to him. She made the Beast believe she wanted his touch, which only confused him and made the act less gratifying.

Beauty knew that she could never escape the Beast, but she could become someone he did not desire enough to torment. She rationalized that if the Beast grew bored with her, he would find another victim. Then, she and the Princess could be free.

Beauty changed into something she was not. She lashed out at the Beast, broke his "rules" and a shift in power dynamics started to happen. The Beast started to react in different ways. He became quiet. The rape was less frequent which meant she had to pretend less often. Inside, Beauty delighted in thinking her plan was working. Her days were spent with her beautiful daughter, basking in the honeymoon of motherhood.

The Princess was perfect. She never cried and slept through the night from the beginning. Beauty felt blessed in so many ways. The Beast was there, but Beauty ignored him, and he seemed to do the same. She believed her plan was working. She fell into a routine of trying to enjoy her happiness while pretending the Beast did not exist. For a little while, it worked. For a time, she found her own little piece of Camelot. But like all her joy, Beauty felt the Beast would take that from her as well, the first chance he gets.

Two months passed before the Beast made his first move to break Beauty's newfound will. While she was basking in her happiness, he had been busy plotting; biding his time and letting the jealousy and monstrous intentions grow inside him. His naïve, little Beauty had no idea of the plans he had for her... but she would soon.

His interest in Beauty seemed to be waning, but the Beast always believed he could have whatever he wanted. Beauty and the Princess would always be his, even when he did not want to play with them. Even if he had other playthings to momentarily divert his attention. No stupid woman would ever best the Beast at his games. He felt it was time to call in a little assistance with his defiant Beauty and enlisted the help of his sister. It would spice things up to have his most trusted ally there to help him break his Beauty once again.

His sister was, after all, quite good at one thing. Drama! She was the Queen of it. Naïve Beauty mistook his actions as change. How easily she had allowed the distraction of a child to make her forget.

He waited months before he showed her his

true face.

6

Something wicked this way comes...

When Beauty's sister-in-law came to live with them, Beauty thought that she would help deter some of the Beast's angry outbursts. She seemed so nice and genuine. Apparently, manipulation was an inherited family trait. Beauty believed his sister would be a balm since he was always complaining about how far away his family was and how much he needed them. She had been so wrong to think of her as an ally. She quickly realized that Beast's sister was just as wicked and cruel as he was. She was a mirror image of her Beastly brother and a true Drama Queen.

Beauty began to suspect that he had acquired some of his cruel temperament from the vile sister. The more the Drama Queen spoke of the dysfunction of the Beast's family, the more Beauty began to see how the monster had been molded. The Beastly sister was just as depraved as her brother. She told tales of their cold wicked mother who purposefully withheld love from her children. She said the woman had been a schizophrenic and was miserable with her husband. She delighted in telling Beauty how she and the Beast's mother routinely cheated on her kind husband, with the man her mother truly loved. The Drama Queen would tell her pitiful tales of abandonment and mistreatment with an underlying pleasure. She spoke of their sexually confused father who enjoyed wearing women's clothing and the company of men.

Beauty had no issues with their father's inclinations, but what bothered her were the tales of the father's anger and abuse. The Drama Queen said neither she or the Beast could be blamed for their actions, because they had been made that way by their childhood. They had, after all, been the subject of a talk show focused on abuses and sexual dysfunctions.

Just when Beauty thought she could not be any more shocked by these monsters, something new would come out. The Drama Queen proved to be exactly as her name indicated. Dramatic. Everything was a chore to her. Everything centered around her. She was like gasoline to the Beast's raging fire.

Beauty also became increasingly weary of the Drama Queen's attachment to the Princess. She gazed upon the child as if she wanted to take her and keep her for her own. The Drama Queen often commented about how all she ever wanted in this life was a child. Beauty tried to quash her growing unease with the Drama Queen's fascination with her daughter, but something inside her would not let the feeling pass. Beauty did not trust the Drama Queen, but she wanted to since his sister always admonished the Beast for his abusive behavior toward Beauty. She wanted so badly to have someone who would understand and give her the keys to controlling the Beast... so she could be free.

Just when Beauty thought she and the Princess might have a shot at a normal life, she now had two monsters to contend with.

When the Beast struck out at Beauty, she thought she had been ready. She was not. It had all started so innocently. He had been dis-pleased with something minor and Beauty ig-nored his ire. In reaction, the Beast went out to drink with his friends. This was never good. Beauty worried for her safety, but the Drama Queen was there. Surely, he would not go over-board with her in the house. Again, Beauty was wrong. The Drama Queen proved to be a babysitter for the Princess, when the Beast de-cided to make his move.

The Beast returned from his night-out in a rage. The Drama Queen took the child and spir-ited her away to her room. The Beast advanced on Beauty, and she tried to run, but when he caught her, she knew all semblance of normality was over and she was back with the old familiar brutality.

The next morning, the Drama Queen smirked at a limping Beauty. The look re-minded her so much of the Beast. That one look told Beauty everything she needed to know about the Drama Queen. She was indeed the same as the Beast. Blood of his blood. Cruelty of his cruelty. A monster in her own right.

A new life emerged for Beauty. One like the one she had during the pregnancy, but now with the two new additions. One, her beloved

Princess who brought her joy. The other, her sister-in-law whom she loathed.

The Drama Queen was pure darkness and hedonistic intentions. She and the Beast were the most depraved creatures Beauty had ever beheld. Beauty had her suspicions that the Drama Queen enjoyed the abuse and took pleasure in her pain... just as the Beast did. Beauty began to fall back into despair, her hopes vanishing with each passing day of brutality. She had to return to work and pretend life was normal, while a viper lived in her home and tried to become surrogate mother to her child. She was cursed by the vile family. All the adults had some sort of depraved inclinations. An innate cruelty, or sexual issues, and were abusive in nature. Beauty did not understand any of them.

For a time, she had tried to understand the Beast and help him. But with time, she realized that she could not understand madness such as his. Nor did she want to. Worse, she had the female version of him living with her as well. Leeching off her financially, finding pleasure in her pain, and trying to steal her child.

Beauty felt cracks in her soul began to widen and her own version of madness seeped out. She began to find comfort in the small dis-comforts of the Beast and Drama Queen. They had opened a chasm in her soul that made her revel in their pains. If the Beast was injured at work, Beauty pretended she cared. She pre-tended to have sympathy, but deep inside... she smiled. When the Drama Queen –who also turned out to be quite promiscuous– caught more than one sexually transmitted disease from a local crackhead she had been sleeping with, well, Beauty felt no sympathy. She did not smile inside because at the time, she would not wish a lifelong case of herpes on anyone.

Beauty just felt numb to the drama. She got so used to living in it with these monsters that nothing surprised or phased her. That was until the day the Drama Queen turned on the Beast, and they had an all-out war.

Beauty did not know what started the war, but she watched the violence and madness from the sidelines. The Drama Queen fought back. Beauty was astounded. Now, granted she was much larger than Beauty and always had that scary, older sister thing she held over the Beast, but Beauty never believed he would allow her to hit him. He did not allow it for long. He started hitting and dragging the Drama Queen from the house. He dragged her through the yard and out of the white picket fence that surrounded the house. Yes, Beauty had a white picket fence, sadly.

The local law enforcement was called by the neighbors and the Drama Queen tried to have the Beast arrested for assault. Another astounding turn for Beauty. Police were against the Beast's rules. Beauty suspected that jail could be the only thing the Beast truly feared.

In the end, the Drama Queen was instructed to leave by the police, and no charges were pressed. This was the day Beauty got to witness the Beast working the system. She realized he could truly talk his way out of anything and avoid going to jail. Even with his sister bleeding and bruised, because he had been removing her from his property. He was within his rights. That was the first time Beauty saw a flaw in the justice system, and the first time she realized all her beliefs about *serve and protect* did not apply to her.

7

My, what big teeth you have...

Beauty became accustomed to a life of fearful anticipation and pain. During her first year with the Beast, she had gone through a myriad of emotions and rationalizations. A constant battle raged inside her. She tried to understand how a person could claim to love her but still hurt her in so many ways. She was caught in a life she did not want but had eventually accepted. She felt shame over her acceptance but told herself it was what it was. This was her life and she held on to a hope that the Boy she had first met might return.

E.L. DUBOIS

The Beast would hurt her and then show kindness, which only reinforced Beauty's fool-hearted hopes. He would apologize and be tender. Those honeymoon periods were always wrought with a futile hope, and a feeling of anticipation for the next time. She took life day by day and found comfort in the only joy she knew. Her little princess, who she spent less and less time with. Beauty worked and was gone most of the day, but she had started to relinquish the caring of her child to her mother, the Queen, more often. She did not want the Princess to hear or bear witness to any of the Beast's tortures, so she let the baby spend more time with her grandmother. It broke Beauty's heart, but she thought it was the only way to shield her child from the monstrous actions of the Beast.

Beauty found that time seemed to pass quickly in the endless cycle her life had become. Constant fighting followed by glimpses of the Boy she hoped still existed within the Beast. During this time, Beauty could feel the tiniest sliver of her mind being frayed. Her emotions running high and low amidst the constant drama were taking their toll on her sanity. Nothing was ever good enough for the Beast. He made her feel as if she would never be enough, even though she cowed to his every whim and tried to please him.

Beauty did not understand her need to please the Beast, but it was constant and a source of torment. All she wanted was to be loved and treated with respect. The Beast would give her tiny pieces of what she sought to keep her in his clutches, but ultimately, all that mattered was what the Beast wanted. She tried with all of her being to be enough for him. She became whatever she thought he needed or wanted. Good Wife, Victim, Lover, Money-Maker, Possession. She did not know why or when she had become this thing, but it had happened, and she was trapped within. It was like being at the center of a beautiful storm with debris swirling all around her. Living in constant fear that she would be devoured, but unable to move from her spot within it. A hope always present in her heart, that the storm would one day pass, and sunlight would peak through. She longed to feel the sunlight on her face once again and did everything she could think of to achieve that calm, but it never came. She convinced herself that she just had to try harder... so she did.

Time passed so quickly that before she knew it, the Beast's birthday was approaching. It would be the second they'd spend together and the first with the Princess. Beauty knew that she had to make each birthday as grand as possible for the Beast. He made it difficult for her, but the need to please the Beast pushed her to try.

Like all holidays, Beauty did her best to be happy about it. That was just her way. Even if she was dying inside, she smiled for the world and tried to make everyone happy. Especially the Beast. She wanted to celebrate the Beast's special day, but he always managed to ruin every holiday. The presents were never enough, the amount of love and appreciation shown him were never enough. This lack of gratitude extended from Beauty to her family. No matter how much money was spent, or kindness was shown, the Beast hated Beauty's family. He had managed to pull them into his manipulations. Beauty witnessed as the King, Queen, and Prince, did things to please the Beast. Buying him presents, including him in family functions, anything to make him feel special and included in their family. The Beast despised every attempt. He would complain that they were not his family and all their kindness was false. They were nothing but fakes. When he was the fake one. He would smile and act as if he was entitled to their gifts. As if he expected that the world and everyone in it owed him something.

Beauty knew that with each approaching holiday, two things would happen. The Beast would provoke an argument that would end in her torture. The honeymoon phase would last through the holiday, and then the Beast would become distraught and the violence would return. The day before the Beast's Birthday, Beauty waited. She anticipated violence, but the Beast deviated from his usual cycle. Instead of hurting Beauty physically or sexually, he crushed her emotionally. She was standing in the kitchen that evening, tired from a long day at work and the stress of anticipation when the Beast walked in and said to her, "I don't love you. I never have. I am not in love with you like that. I care for you because you are the mother of my child... but nothing more."

Beauty crumpled to the floor in tears. Through all the pain, the Beast had never hurt her as badly as he did with that declaration.

The Beast leaned his back against the wall across from her and slid down to watch as she cried. His gaze was intense but devoid of emotion. He probably thought she was crying because she couldn't stand to know he did not love her. The truth is, she didn't know why. All she knew was that she had never felt a pain like the one ripping through her.

Maybe she cried because she felt like a failure.

Maybe she cried because she had tried so hard and it was all for nothing.

She had lost so many pieces of her soul and given up so much of herself to the Beast and it still had meant nothing. The pain she had endured had no purpose.

Maybe she cried because part of her did love the Beast.

Maybe she cried because his words had snapped the final cord of her remaining hope.

Beauty just did not know why the tears and sobs were racking her body. All she knew in that moment was a new and different kind of pain. It was a wrongness. A hurt like no other and she wanted to claw it from her body and never experience it again.

Through the gut-wrenching agony, Beauty feebly asked the Beast, "You were NEVER in love with me? Not once? Not even a little? You never felt that kind of love for me? After everything?"

The Beast's response was a flat "No." Then, he left her to cry on the floor.

At some point, she picked herself up and tended to the Princess. She still felt the wrongness of that agony, but she plastered on her smile and loved her little girl. With time and the presence of her daughter, her mind emptied itself of all questions, and a numbness replaced the agony.

She went through the motions that evening like it was no different from any other. The Beast acted as if he had never said anything and ignored Beauty. She served him his dinner, put the baby down and retired to bed. The Beast joined her but never touched her. He turned his back to her as if she didn't exist. This threw Beauty. That agony began to creep back as she lay in the dark, listening to the Beast's even breathing.

Beauty sank deeper and deeper with each passing hour. Her very existence became a tailspin of emotional despair. Her mind whirling with so many questions as the time ticked by. She could deal with the physical pain, but his rejection was unbearable. She toyed with the idea that she had loved the Beast in her own way after all.

Could fear morph into love, the way love had morphed into fear? She had to have loved him, right? Why else would she have given herself so completely to him? Why would she let herself be subjected to such awful pain and degradation if not for love?

She felt as if it had all been for nothing because she was nothing to the Beast. Not even a possession anymore. He was tired of her and she was just a plaything that had now been discarded. She silently cried herself to sleep that night.

When Beauty awoke the next morning, the Beast was gone. There was no *good morning, I love you* text. No, *I miss you, what are you doing?* text. No dozens of missed calls. No contact at all. No obsessive behavior. Beauty did not know how to feel. She was so mentally and emotionally exhausted.

Her pain gave her some clarity and a newfound sense of reality. Hadn't she wanted the Beast to discard her? She and the Princess could be free. When had the hate she felt turn into a need for his love? She felt so confused but knew without a doubt what she had to do. She had to

leave. If a Beast with no tenderness or possibility of love was all that she had, then her life
could only get worse.

Beauty planned, and she called the Queen.
She told her mother what the Beast had said,
and her mother made arrangements for Beauty.
The Queen would set up for Beauty and the
Princess to stay at a hotel in a town, about thirty
miles from their home. Everything would be in
the Queen's name, so the Beast could not trace
it and find them.

Beauty packed a bag for her and the Princess. Then, she wrote the Beast a letter. In it, she
told him all the things she had never had the
courage to say. She told him how badly he had
hurt her. How she wished he had left her and
never abused her. She told him how foolish she
felt to love someone like him, who had never
loved her back. She told him many things and it
felt freeing to finally be honest. As she left their
home and headed to the hotel, Beauty could not
shake her pain. She did not understand why she
was hurting. When had she really fallen in love
with the Beast? Why would she want to still be
with him? Why didn't she want this torture to
be over? Why wasn't she happy to be free of
him? Why did she seek the approval and love of

a Beast? What was wrong with her? Had the Beast driven her insane?

These were the constant thoughts that plagued her as she checked into the hotel, and she and the Princess settled into their temporary home. Beauty was feeling so many things at once as she watched the beautiful Princess sleeping. She had come from a family where her parents were still together. She believed that if you had a child with someone, you made it work. But neither her mother or father had been a Beast... so maybe she was wrong.

Just when Beauty was beginning to feel as though she had truly been fighting a losing battle, her cell phone began to ring. It was the Beast. He had obviously returned home. Beauty did not answer. She simultaneously felt a spike of fear and something else. Was that happiness that he cared enough to call? She let the phone ring as he called back to back. His obsessive behavior was back in full force. Apology text messages came, followed by angry ones with threats. He left threatening voice messages, and ones with tears, proclaiming he never meant what he said. He professed that he had been scared and thought he was losing Beauty. That he loved her more than life and could not live without her and the baby. He promised that he was in love with her and not just because they had a child. He said all the things that Beauty did not realize she wanted to hear. This was another form of the honeymoon cycle... she just did not realize it. She should've, after all this time. He loved to inflict terrible pain, followed by tenderness.

Beauty's fear outweighed her other feelings, because she did not want to experience violence again. She did not answer the Beast. She listened to one final message before turning off her phone. In the message, the Beast had sounded distraught. He told Beauty he was going to his mother's because he did not want to be alone and that he truly loved her. Not knowing what to make of this one hundred and eighty degree turn in the Beast's behavior, Beauty decided to ignore it all for the moment. She just wanted to feel nothing again after all the drama, so she settled down to watch mindless television as the baby slept.

That's why when there was a knock at the door thirty minutes later, Beauty thought it was her mother. It was not. She opened the door to find the Beast.

He was teetering on the brink of insanity.

Beauty could see the crazy brimming from him. She took a step back and he stepped inside, shutting the door behind him. A stunned Beauty asked the Beast what he was doing there. How had he found them?

The Beast told Beauty that if she was going to run, she would need to do a better job of it. He had to pass through the town she was in on his way to his mother's and had seen Beauty's car in the hotel parking lot. He only had to knock on two other doors before finding her.

She felt so stupid and afraid. She did not know what to do with this Beast. She could not read him. She did not know what he intended. As he advanced on her, she stepped back until the backs of her knees hit the bed. She did not want violence in the same room as the Princess. She had been able to prevent that before now. Her eyes pleaded with the Beast and he raised his hand to her. She tensed, waiting for a blow, but it never came. Instead, the Beast wrapped his arms around her and cried. She was shell-shocked. The Beast was rocking and crying, and murmuring into her hair, saying that when he thought he had lost her, it hit him how much he did love her and could not live without her. He told her how frightened he had been to lose his little family. He promised to try harder and be someone she deserved. He even gazed at the Princess with what looked like sincere love and promised to be a better father to her as well.

The Beast gently laid Beauty on the bed and tenderly engulfed her in his arms. Beauty did not know what to say or do. She had been on a razor's edge of emotions and pain for so long, this version of the Beast was throwing her for a loop. Maybe not the Beast? Was that her Boy she was seeing? Was that who she loved and longed for? The kind and gentle boy who had shown her such passion and tenderness in the beginning?

It was then Beauty realized that maybe she was holding on for the Boy she loved. She was forever optimistic that the Boy would return. In all the Beast's moments of tenderness, it had not been the Beast at all. It had been the Boy. Maybe he was trapped by the Beast, just like she was.

If Beauty could only help the Boy defeat his demon Beast, then they could all be happy. She could be loved by the father of her child. The Princess would not come from a broken home and the Boy would truly love her as Beauty did. All Beauty had to do was find a way to bring out the Boy more often, and defeat the Beast, then they could have their happily ever after.

As exhaustion and the Boy's warmth and deep gentle voice overtook Beauty, she decided to hold on to her Boy and never let go. Their happiness depended on her. She would defeat the Beast or die trying.

8

Not your Mamma's fairy-tale...

The queen was livid with Beauty for going back to the Beast. She told her daughter time after time that, "she had been raised better." The Queen hated the Beast and did not understand why Beauty stayed with him. Beauty knew her mother was only concerned, but every time she questioned Beauty, it only made her feel like a weak-willed girl.

Over the next couple of months, a change happened. The Beast lay dormant. When Beauty left the Beast, a miracle had happened. The Boy returned. She was wary at first, always waiting for the Beast to rear his ugly head... but he didn't. The Boy was gentle and sweet. He loved Beauty and the Princess so fiercely that the hope inside Beauty returned full force and blossomed.

During this time, the Boy took a job traveling. He said he did it for the family, and the raise in pay could improve their lives. He even got to work with his best friend and some friends from his childhood. The Boy seemed truly happy, so Beauty thought she was as well. She tried to put all the wrong of the past behind her and embrace her present. She was spending more time with the Princess, and when the Boy was home, times were good. The Princess even had her first birthday and the Beast never showed. It was the first holiday the Beast had not ruined. It seemed like life was turning around.

Then, the Princess got sick. The Boy was home from a work-trip but would be leaving that evening for another. He was watching the Princess while Beauty was at work. The Queen came by to see the Princess and noticed she felt feverish. The Queen asked the Boy if he had checked the Princess's temperature and he had not. When the Queen checked, the little girl had a fever of 103.5. The Queen immediately called Beauty and took the Princess to the hospital. Beauty left work right away and raced to be with her child.

Since the child had no visible signs of sickness, the Queen did not know what was wrong with the baby. The Doctor's found the source of the Princess's sickness when they checked her diaper. She had a golf ball sized abscess on one of her bottom cheeks. The Queen and Beauty had never seen anything like it. The Doctor explained that it was very dangerous, and the baby needed to be transferred to a children's hospital right away for emergency surgery. Beauty was more frightened than she had ever been. The thought of her child being sick and needing surgery was devastating. The Boy acted unworried. He comforted Beauty and told her their daughter would be fine. She tried to figure out how he could be so calm, but she had other, more pressing concerns in mind.

On an early summer morning before dawn, the Princess underwent surgery. The Doctors removed the abscess and placed drains in her bottom. They told Beauty it was a very bad and contagious Staff Infection. She had no clue where the baby could have gotten the infection. She had not been in any kind of day care. The Doctors told Beauty that anyone could have brought it in their shoes, and not to blame herself.

The Princess was put on strong antibiotics and released to Beauty for care at home. Beauty was relieved that it was nothing more serious. The Boy still acted unconcerned and went straight to work. He seemed more worried about not spending time with his friends than the Princess's health. Beauty could tell something was off with him but was too worried about the Princess to care.

Three days later, when Beauty had barely heard from the Boy, her suspicions were confirmed. Instead of returning home to be with his wife and daughter, or to care for his daughter during her illness, he sent Beauty a text message that he needed some space and would be living with his best friend. Beauty was devastated at first. She thought things were better. The Beast went away, and the Boy had returned. How could anyone abandon their child while they were sick?

Once the shock wore off, Beauty got pissed. No longer a simpering, wilting flower, she told the Coward Boy exactly what she thought of him and good riddance. Seriously, after all the crap he had put her through, all he could manage was a text message? What a spineless wimp.

She began to feel a certain freedom return. Yes, the Boy was gone, but so was any worry of the Beast returning. Within two weeks, Beauty had taken a new job and moved. She found a nice little place in an upscale, gated community for her and the Princess. She was farther away from her family, but she had a new sense of wanting to start over – just her and the Princess. She wanted to make it on her own.

Beauty believed she was exactly where she needed to be to have a better life. She and the Princess had made it through the storm and were on the other side.

Since the Boy was being civil and obviously did not want Beauty, she thought they were safe. He seemed unconcerned with anything that had to do with Beauty and his child. She had her suspicions. He might have a new victim, so his obsession with her had probably shifted to someone else.

The Boy contacted Beauty offering financial help for the Princess and to talk about visitation. Beauty allowed the Boy to visit them and bring money, diapers, and milk. Whatever the baby needed. He showed no indication of the Beast or any intention toward Beauty, other than civility for the child's sake. Therefore, after a month on their own, Beauty thought it was safe to meet the Boy.

The Queen had visited Beauty and was watching the Princess while Beauty was at work. The Boy had texted Beauty asking her to come by his friend's house because he had money for her. When Beauty asked why he could not drop it off, he told her he was having issues with his truck. Beauty thought, "no big deal." His friend's house was on the way home.

Since the Queen was staying over and helping with the Princess, Beauty made plans to meet a friend. It had been such a long time since she had been out, and she just wanted adult conversation and to catch up. Beauty let the Boy know she would stop by, but first she had plans, so she would meet him after. The Boy told her he would be leaving soon, and no one would be home for a few days. Beauty did not want to deal with the Boy's drama, so she agreed to spare a few minutes on her way out and grab the money. The Boy agreed. It was a simple conversation. Beauty felt no worry.

She had let her guard down around the Boy. That was her first mistake. She would never make it to dinner with her friend that night.

9

Along came a spider who sat down beside her...

Whenever the boy was present for long periods of time, Beauty would forget how closely the Beast lurked beneath the mask of the Boy. In the beginning, it had caused many of her downfalls. It took her years to realize that the Boy was the illusion... not the Beast.

That night, she went to meet the Boy with no fear of the Beast. She had a newfound confidence in herself and in his lack of interest in her. So, when the Boy invited her into the friend's house, Beauty agreed but only for a minute.

When the friend and his wife waved at her as she passed through their living room, she thought, "Oh good, we are not alone. Not that I should worry, but still good."

Even as she followed the Boy to his room, she did not feel the tingling sense of alarm she would have had six months earlier.

It was not until she entered the room and heard the Boy click the lock on his door into place, did that old familiar sense of dread creep back in. She stood motionless, saying nothing for several seconds. Beauty was trying to process why the Boy had locked the door. She had just opened her mouth to protest, when strong arms wrapped around her from behind. A shiver went down her spine, and her body tensed, as an all too familiar voice whispered in her ear, "Did you really think I would let you go?"

It was the Beast. Beauty fought against his grip but her struggles only ignited his lust. He covered her mouth when she tried to scream and panic began to set in. Her fight or flight response kicked in and Beauty wanted to fight and flee. She bit down hard on the Beast's hand, which brought her a yelp of pain and a backhand across the face. The Beast had actually hit her in the face. He cursed her as she kicked and cried out. As they struggled, he threw her onto the bed and began yanking her clothes off. Beauty tried to get away. She clawed and fought like never before, but it was all for nothing.

As the Beast violated her over and over, she started to disconnect from herself and what was happening. There was a strange sensation like she was floating and watching the brutality happen to someone she did not know.

The Beast was more brutal sexually than he had ever been. No one heard her cries. No one came to her rescue. When he was done, she was still in a daze. The Beast told her that she would always be his. There was no escape. She thought she could go out with someone else? He would never be replaced.

Beauty did not register the absurdity of his accusations. She was not trying to date anyone else. The Beast sat beside her for what could have been minutes or hours, murmuring all the horrible threats and plans he had for her. He had been plotting all these months and the Beast would be satisfied. Beauty must have been in shock, because she registered none of it. Her only thoughts were absurd ones. She thought about work. She thought about the weather.

What she did not do was think about what had just been done to her or how her new life was about to change, again.

She stayed unmoving, like a vacant shell, even as he dressed her. She did not respond as he walked her outside to her car. She did not register the friend or his wife, who had to have heard but did nothing.

Beauty did not utter a word until after the Beast grasped her face and kissed it. He told her to text him and let him know she made it home safe. She only nodded. When the Beast acted un-pleased with that response, she croaked out a feeble yes.

Beauty did not remember the drive home. She did not remember the walk to her door or the brief conversation with the Queen in her darkened living room. What she did remember was the blood. She had to wash the Beast from her body and there was so much blood from the brutality. She remembered the pain as the numbness and shock wore off.

Beauty remembered the tears.

She cried silent tears for what the Beast had done to her and still planned to do.

She cried silent tears over her stupidity.

She cried silent tears until she fell asleep.

Her tears were silent because she was so ashamed for being such a fool. She did not want the Queen to know what the Beast had done to her.

10

Huff and puff and blow the house down...

T he next day, the Beast moved into Beauty's home and proclaimed it his. For two weeks, he enacted bouts of bru- tality followed by glimmers of tenderness. All his actions still confused Beauty. She had never known another who acted like the Beast.

The Queen found out the Beast was living with Beauty and treated her with disgust and disdain. The Queen loved Beauty but did not understand how her daughter could be so weak to take the Beast back. She had no idea of the torments Beauty endured and the feeling of loss, as her mother drifted further away, sending Beauty into a deeper despair.

Beauty was losing herself in so many ways. She did not understand how she could allow the Beast to hurt her and still feel as if his brand of normal was now her own.

The first few months of his arrival back into their lives was wrought with so many emotions. She had started a new job and had to learn it. She could barely function at work and held her façade of normal intact the best that she could. At home, she lived a nightmare. The Beast seemed more distracted and angry all the time. She could see a massive storm brewing within the Beast and did her best to survive. He appeared so unhappy to be back with Beauty, but his obsession with her had magnified. His actions were a contradiction to her and nothing made sense.

Father's Day came, and Beauty dreaded the holiday. She had to put on a false face. Somewhere along the grueling path of life with the Beast, Beauty had adorned her own glass mask. Instead of hiding a monster, she hid a frightened, tortured, and trapped young woman.

The day went as expected, catering to his

wants and needs. Trips to various vile family members that Beauty could barely stomach. They were all so fake to Beauty and she could sense in them that same underlying falseness the Beast embodied.

As the day ended and they headed home, the Beast's anger bubbled over during the car ride. He began driving at high speeds, screaming and acting erratically. Beauty was frightened for the Princess who was in her car seat at the back of the vehicle. The Princess cried as the Beast screamed. At one point, he skidded the vehicle to a stop, leaped out of the car and rounded it to Beauty's side. With a quick jerk of the door, he was inside and in her face, screaming at the top of his lungs. The sound was deafening to Beauty. She cried and cowered in fear as he jerked her hair and assaulted her on the side of a busy intersection. After momentarily sating his lust for violence, he got back into the vehicle and continued the drive home. All the while berating Beauty. He told her she was nothing, a Bitch who deserved everything she got. He said he treated her like this because she did not love him enough or in the right way. The insults were endless and meant to cut away any self-esteem Beauty had left. Beauty cried with force. The gut-wrenching cries of a woman on the verge of breaking. Beast was trying to break her. She hated to let him see her cry these kinds of tears. She hated to let him see the soul-searing pain he could inflict upon her, because she knew that these were the true moments that brought him the most pleasure. If he could push her to that point, he would do it repeatedly. It was a drug to him. He fed off it like the addict he was. It made the Beast high to have so much control over Beauty.

The Beast had many addictions. He was always seeking a high of some sort; from drugs, sex, and abuse. Anything and everything that gave him a rush. In that moment, in that car, Beauty realized something very important. She was another addiction to the Beast. Her pain was the ultimate high for him.

When they finally arrived home, the tsunami of anger only magnified. Beauty could almost see it dancing around him like black smoke tendrils; a real-life manifestation of the pain he was about to inflict. She managed to get the Princess tucked away in her room, to shield her daughter from the monster. The car ride had been bad enough. She had been powerless to protect her and only prayed the baby was too young to ever remember the brutality of the Beast.

Beauty knew the days were numbered on how long she could shield the Princess, and silently prayed for a miracle as she put her daughter down to sleep. The Princess was so lovely and small. The only ray of hope in Beauty's life. She did not want to leave her side. She did not want to face the monster just beyond her daughter's door, but she could hear him pacing. Waiting... stalking... like a caged predator for his prey. If Beauty did not go out to the Wolf at her door, he would bring it down.

Resigned to her fate and with a heavy heart, Beauty silently left the Princess's sleeping form and went to face her fate. The Beast immediately pounced on her. His abuses quiet and menacing. Beauty suffered in silence so no one would hear. Not the baby, not the neighbors. When the Beast was sated, Beauty lay curled into a ball in the corner. Her clothes were torn. Her body was battered, and she bled from her most intimate places. Beauty thought the Beast was done, his lusts sated, but she was wrong. He had only gotten the physical and sexual torture out of the way. As he approached, she instinctively moved closer to the wall and away from him.

With a sneer, he grasped her chin and said, "How does my Beauty feel?"

She answered him honestly, her voice barely above a whisper. "You are breaking me. You are breaking my heart with this."

A broad smile spread across the Beast's face and he laughed, a low, menacing sound that made the hairs on Beauty's nape rise. His voice was the personification of evil.

"Oh, my sweet, ignorant little Beauty. Heartbreaking? You want heartbreaking? I got some heartbreaking shit for you." Then, the Beast pulled out his cell phone and dialed a number. Beauty found his behavior odd and watched as he asked the person on the other line, "Can I come to your house?"

Beauty did not know what to make of the Beast. He had changed into a normal person for that single-sentence conversation. When he hung up, he sneered down at Beauty one last time, turned his back on her, grabbed his keys from the counter and walked out the door. He never looked back and she laid on the floor, her face pressed to the cool tile, and cried until it felt like she had no more tears left.

When Beauty was finally able to stand, she

made her way to the bathroom to clean up. Before her bath, she stared for a long time at the naked reflection of the creature in the mirror. Her long, raven hair was a tangled mess, matted with blood. Her body was starting to bruise in places. She had a large, purpling spot on her left thigh. Bite marks and scratches riddled the skin of her breasts, torso and upper arms. Her eyes were swollen and puffy. Nose red, cheeks flushed, but it was unmarked and still beautiful. Her ribs and left shoulder hurt so badly. The shoulder hung at an unnatural angle and Beauty realized it had been dislocated. She knew how to relocate it herself from previous injuries, so she gritted her teeth and tried to relax. She bent her elbow, cradled her forearm and tried to rotate it back into place. It did not want to budge so she eventually had to use a more forceful approach. Once it was back in place, she cleaned the blood and the Beast from her body. Once dressed, she took over-the-counter pain relievers and got some ice. She did not eat. She rarely ate anymore. Her body was becoming gaunt and frailer with each day. The stress was making her lose weight rapidly. A moment of worry crept in as she remembered the Beast's comments about her weight loss.

First, he had praised her, then he had warned her that she'd better not lose too much. He liked his women with nice round asses and her breasts were already too small. The emotional scars were ever present even when he was not.

Beauty fed the Princess and laid in bed with her. The numbness started to seep in and Beauty was overtaken by exhaustion. The house was silent except for the Princess's breathing. The sweet rhythm lulled Beauty into a dreamless land, her cherished daughter cradled in her good arm.

The Beast did not return that night or even the next morning. Beauty hoped he would not return at all. That evening, all her hopes were dashed when she saw his truck parked in front of her home. When she unlocked the door, the babysitter had gone, and Beast bounced the Princess as she giggled. He looked happy and was planning to cook dinner. All Beauty could do was gape at him.

The Princess reached out to her and she took the sweet child into her good arm. The Beast embraced them both and smiled broadly. He was so chipper, Beauty wanted to vomit. This false display of happiness had become grotesque to her.

The Beast whispered in her ear, "I am so glad you are home. Now I have both my girls. I have missed you so much. Go get changed and relax. I will take care of dinner."

Beauty eyed him suspiciously but took the baby with her as she changed out of her work clothes. She was silent as she entered the kitchen and saw the Beast smiling as he texted on his phone. She said nothing and just watched him. When the baby made a noise, he was startled. Like a kid caught with his hand in the cookie jar. Beauty knew the Beast was up to something with someone. All his recent and constant accusations of infidelity began to make perfect sense.

She said nothing and just walked to the couch and sat down. Her thoughts were a jumbled mess that evening as she started going back over all of his suspicious behavior since the baby had gotten sick. The need to move out. The accusations of infidelity that he used to rape her and move back in on their life. His constant guarding of his cell phone. The ringer never on. He always had it on silent or vibrate.

As she went to bed that night, awake and staring at the ceiling, she wondered how he had the time to try and romance another woman, with all the efforts he put into obsessing over her and making her life miserable.

Around two in the morning, she began to think there was no way he could have had the time. At four that morning, all her suspicions were confirmed. She had gotten out of bed and was getting ready for work. She heard a buzzing coming from the Beast's pants on the floor. She immediately pulled the phone from his pants' pocket and silently slipped into the living room. With a whisper, she answered the phone. A female asked for the Beast.

Beauty said, "May I ask who is calling?"

The female replied, "His girlfriend. Who are you?"

Beauty simply stated, "His wife."

11

All the King's horses, and all the King's men, couldn't put Beauty back together again…

B eauty wanted to throw up and rage against the world as the woman on the other end of the phone apologized, then proceeded to detail all the things she had done with the Beast. After the initial call, Beauty had given the Bar-Wench her phone number and re-turned the Beast's phone to his pocket. When the woman called, she told Beauty the story of how the Beast had picked her up in the bar and how she had slept with him on the first night.

She told Beauty how he had, in fact, come to her house on Father's Day and spent the night. Beauty's head was reeling with every trashy detail and comment the Bar-Wench gave her. The woman went on and on about how she had no idea the Beast was married. He had told her he was divorced. She even told Beauty their daughter was beautiful. This made Beauty pause. The Beast had shown this slut random pictures of their daughter? WTH? The Bar-Wench had no shame, and as Beauty listened, quietly falling deeper into the numbness, she detailed every sexual act she had shared with the Beast.

When Beauty could not bear to hear another word, she told the Bar-Wench exactly what the Beast really was and gave her a few details of her own. She made sure that his hook-up knew he was not some great catch. He was all lies. She told her in a deadened tone how the Beast had beaten and raped Beauty before coming to her house to screw her five times in three hours.

To this, the woman replied, "Oh we did not use any protection. I'm allergic to condoms and not on the pill, but he did not seem to care."

Beauty just gaped. Where in hell did he find

people like this? Oh wait…the Bar. How stupid could this random chick be?

Beauty did not even know what to say anymore. Not only had the Beast put her through hell, raped her, abused her in every way… now he was cheating too. Possibly exposing her to sexually transmitted diseases. WTF! Worst of all, he would not let her go or leave her alone. Beauty hung up on the Bar-Wench while she was in mid-sentence. The sentence started like this, "I'm Catholic. I would never break up a marriage." Beauty did not hear the rest as she hung up. All she thought was, *it's ok to have unprotected sex with some random guy at the Bar, possibly get pregnant or diseases, but not ok if he is married. How very Catholic of you.* Jeez, when had her life become a bad Lifetime movie?

As Beauty sat in her living room watching the sun come up and trying to process all she had been through, something inside her gave way. With a determination like she never felt before, she went and got the Princess and took her to the babysitter. You would think she would flee, but that snap had been years of anger and abuse. She wanted to fight back. She wanted retribution for all the Beast had done to her. So, her next step was to call work and tell them she would be late that day. Then, she drove home, ready for an epic battle.

When she returned home, the Beast was still sleeping. Beauty took advantage of that fact and channeled Angela Bassett from Waiting to Exhale. Damn the consequences. This son of a bitch had it coming. Seriously though, he was a true S.O.B. in every sense of the word. If you ever met her Mother-in-law, the Wicked Bitch of the West, you would understand.

The Beast awoke as Beauty was methodically throwing all his shit out of the second story balcony. Something in her eyes must have given him pause because he did not try to attack her. He just stood there watching Beauty go completely and utterly nuts on a nuclear level. When he came near her, it was like he was approaching a wild animal. Beauty had never acted or felt like she was losing complete control until that morning. All his abuse and betrayals had mounted up and overflowed. She was not a violent person by nature, but that day, when he attempted to restrain her, she kicked, clawed, and punched the Beast as hard as she could. He only tried to restrain her once before backing off. She screamed and raged as he watched her. She felt no fear. She only felt rage. The adrenaline coursing through her veins made her feel like she had the strength of ten men. It was both exhilarating and frightening. She felt crazed. She felt insane. The Beast had made her crazy. WTF was happening to her?

She was sobbing and breathing heavily when she finally slid down the wall and hung her head between her knees. She was so exhausted – physically, mentally, emotionally. Was this how the Beast felt after he lashed out at her? Was this the high and low he was constantly chasing? Beauty did not understand anything anymore.

She was not sure how long she sat there panting, before the Beast approached. When she slowly brought her hazel eyes up to meet his ice blue ones, she saw no anger or remorse. She only saw pleasure and amusement in them. Why was she not surprised? This muthafucka…

12

Why, sometimes I've believed as many as six impossible things before breakfast...

The Beast was only wearing low-slung jeans and no shirt. Probably because his other clothing was all over the yard and his truck, which Beauty had contemplated setting on fire, but her rage had fizzled out before she got there.

The Beast slowly crouched down, resting his forearm on Beauty's knees. He never broke eye contact. They stared at each other for a long time. He seemed to be searching her eyes and face for the reason behind her snap. Beauty knew the exact moment he figured it out, because a wide smile spread across his face. She wanted to claw out his eyes, and her fingers clenched in response. This amused the Beast. His perfect white teeth and tanned skin mocked her. The sparkle in those cold blue eyes was sickening. Beauty did not move or flinch as the Beast leaned his face close enough to hers that their breaths mingled. She could feel excitement coming off him and a feeling of unease began to creep up her spine.

His deep southern drawl was low and amused. "I see my Beauty has found out about my new darling."

Without even realizing she had done it, Beauty slapped the Beast across his face so hard a crack echoed through the eerily silent house, and her hand stung like a thousand bees had attacked her palm. The action had whipped the Beast's head to one side. A stunned Beauty tensed and readied herself for retaliation. But the Beast merely turned to her, smiling. She caught a flash of fire in those cold eyes. The blood from his split lip making his teeth a grotesque sight. Then, the Beast did the last thing Beauty expected. He let out a long, exuberant laugh. The kind of belly laugh that made him clutch his abdomen and fall back on his butt.

When he finally stopped laughing, his words were cold and callous, "I did not know if I was in love with you. So, I went looking for a confirmation. She looks a lot like you, but she has bigger breasts and likes to do drugs with me. I thought that made her like you, but only better."

Beauty was seething inside but made her response cold and flat as she stood to leave. "Then go be with the Bar-Wench. Your better version of me. I want you gone before I get home."

Beauty did not even make it to the door before the Beast was on her. He gripped her by both arms and backed her against the wall. His demeanor was menacing and cold as he placed an arm on either side of her body, caging her in. His face was only inches from hers. She tensed, awaiting his next move. He dipped his head and slowly ran his nose against her neck, breathing in scent. His words were a mere whisper by her ear.

"Want to know what I learned? She was not better than you. No one is better than you. You are perfect for me and I know that now. If you just had bigger breasts or were not against my drug use, this would never have happened. She was your fault. But, I know now that you are the one, Beauty. My perfect possession, even with your shortcomings. I will never find a more perfect plaything. I just had to confirm that and now it's over with. It will never happen again. I want no one else. I need no one else, because I have you. My Beauty. I will always have you and you will always be mine. I will never let you go, because I will never allow you to carry another man's child, and I will never allow another man to be father to the Princess. You and her belong to me. I am not going anywhere. Do you hear me? YOU ARE MINE! So, be a good little Beauty and go get into the car. I will be driving you to work from now on. I will forgive this kind of behavior this one time and I will see you when I pick you up."

Beauty was trembling from his tone and words. She wanted him gone with every fiber of her being. Instead, he was staying and giving her orders. As he lightly kissed her cheek and patted her on the butt, he opened the door. Her thoughts were a whirlwind. The gall of him after all he had done. To betray and hurt her so easily and then blame her? Good God, what had she done to deserve this?

The Beast was evolving right before her into an even more heinous monster. One who played with her life and emotions like she was his pawn in a chess game. She was trapped in a never-ending, evolving cycle of emotional, physical, sexual pain, and the only way she might ever escape is through death.

Either her death, or his.

13

Lift your head, Beauty
If not, the crown falls...

In the days after Beauty found out about the Beast's infidelity, she began to unravel. The days of her driving had been revoked. He watched every move she made and monitored all her contact. She had nothing private. He checked her phone, emails and social media. All her passwords had to be accessible and if they were not, Beauty paid with a pound of flesh.

He pretended in front of others that he was remorseful. He had, of course, confessed his heinous acts of infidelity to anyone who would listen. Not because he truly felt bad, but because he wanted others to see Beauty as weak. What kind of woman forgives and stays which such a cad? He never confessed all the other abuses. He never would. Being an adulterer was one thing, but the Beast would never admit to the true monster he was.

The Beast even went as far as to make Beauty attend couple's counseling through his father's church. The ridiculousness just kept piling up. All he cared about was perception. He was a misguided, lustful husband who had betrayed his loving wife but wanted redemption. Beauty look like a weak and ignorant wife who was standing by her deplorable man. The church counseling sessions were the absolute worst for Beauty. All the men and women had known the Beast when he was a child. They all knew the sordid details of his father and ex-stepmother's relationship. His family had no shame and told all their business to anyone who would listen. Hence, the talk show. Every time Beauty had to attend one of the sessions and feel all the pitying eyes upon her, she wanted to yack.

Something inside Beauty woke up that day. Some sense of self-preservation or caring. The

Beast's actions had changed as well. It was like the high off her mental meltdown was sustaining his need for violence.

One day, at work, Beauty became very sick. She was running a very high fever and had a pain in her groin area that was so severe she could not walk. The Beast came and got her after work and took her to the hospital. The doctors told Beauty she had the same kind of infection the Princess had suffered from and would need to be treated with surgery and strong antibiotics. Beauty felt so bad that the Princess had suffered this pain, because Beauty had probably carried the infection in on her shoes. She had surgery and spent the next week in the hospital. The Princess stayed with the Queen because, of course, the Beast was right by her side the entire time.

One day, as Beauty lay in the hospital bed staring at the ceiling, a sweet nurse came in to check her vital signs, so the Beast was on his best behavior. Beauty's phone rang but because the nurse was present, the Beast could not jump up to snatch it from Beauty's hands and field the call. Beauty did not recognize the number, but she answered.

"Hello"

The voice on the other end of the phone made Beauty sick with disgust.

It was the Bar-Wench with her whiny, chipmunk voice.

"I was just calling to let you know I am not pregnant."

Beauty could not believe the gall of the Wench.

"Great, thanks! Never call me again."

Beauty was just about to hang up when the shrill woman's voice stopped her.

"Wait, I just thought you should know I have been in the hospital. I got a staph infection and I think it was from him."

Beauty could feel the blood draining from her face.

She glanced at the Beast. He was charming the nurse with a smile and small talk, but his eyes were on Beauty. She was never out of his sight. Like a small injured animal in his trap. She was his favorite kind of prey.

"Me too," was all she could utter before she hung up.

When the nurse left the room, the Beast quickly lost his mask of politeness.

"Who was that"?

"Your Bar-Wench."

The Beast looked at Beauty expectantly. His expression, one that said, "Don't make me have to ask."

"Congratulations, you are NOT going to be a father."

A moment of relief crossed his face. It was so brief, Beauty almost missed it. If it had been anyone else, they would have missed it... but not Beauty. After a few years with this monster, she could see his tells.

Beauty made her move.

"She had something else interesting to say."

His voice was low, and his eyes narrowed.

"What was that, beautiful?"

Beauty hated when he called her beautiful. She knew he found true beauty in her pain, degradation, and loss of self. It had nothing to do with outside beauty and everything to do with the chaos inside her.

"She said she has been in the hospital with a staph infection, like mine, and she thinks you gave it to her."

The Beast cocked one eyebrow, and the corners of his lips tipped up in a sneer.

"Is that it"? His laugh was hearty and condescending.

"Of course, I gave it to her. I gave it to all

my girls. That kind of thing is all over strip clubs and the nasty strippers that work there. I had it before the Princess got sick and dug it out of my arm myself. I got it from this stripper I messed with before that girl from the bar."

Beauty went completely still. His laugh echoed off the marble floor of the hospital room.

"Oh, Beauty, your face is priceless. I love it. All this time you were blaming yourself and I was laughing inside at my own nasty, little secret. I hoped eventually you would get it and then I could tell you. I love how clueless you are."

Beauty vomited then, right into the pink plastic tub beside her hospital bed. She turned away from the Beast and silent tears fell from her eyes. She cried without making a sound or movement. She had trained herself to cry with even breaths, like she was sleeping, so the Beast would not see her tears. He was still amusing himself and chuckling over his accomplishments when Beauty drifted off to sleep.

Beauty was released from the hospital and the Beast expected her to go back to her daily chores like she had never been sick. There was no recovery time for Beauty. She just had to grit her teeth and bear the pain. That was her life.

The total stability of her instable life ate away at her sanity and Beauty began acting out, purposefully defying the Beast. Not telling him where she was going or answering his obsessive calls and texts. She just wanted to stay away. She wanted freedom from her life with him. It only took two weeks for Beauty to find what she had been looking for.

It was a hot summer day. Beauty wore a tank top and mini-denim skirt with flip-flops. The Beast had invited his brood of buddies over to hang out. He had one set of buddies who were brothers. One brother was notorious for being a handsome ladies' man and made his admiration for Beauty no secret. His looks always lingered a little too long. He would find reasons to touch Beauty or compliment her. He was a false Prince Charming and Hero with no real aspirations for Beauty, and Beauty did not like how his attentions made the Beast react. To his friend, the Beast was all smiles. To Beauty, he was constantly accusing her of wanting to sleep with the False Hero as revenge. He accused Beauty of seeking out the attentions of his friend. Beauty barely even noticed or registered any of the attentions the Beast was accusing her of wanting. The Beast would complain he could have no friends because they all wanted Beauty, which she did not see.

Beauty was so tired of feeling like a caged animal that was constantly being abused, poked, and prodded. The Princess was staying with the Wicked Bitch of the West that day. She hated leaving her child with that woman, but the Beast insisted his mother get to spend time with the Princess. Usually, this meant the wicked woman would spend all her time dressing up and making the Princess pose for photos. The wicked woman fancied herself a photographer and she loved to take pictures of the children, until she deemed them too old to be cute enough anymore. Beauty had witnessed this behavior with the wicked woman's own children, and knew it was only a matter of time until the Witch lost interest in the Princess. The Beast, his family, the constant need to please all of them, was just more punishment that Beauty did not understand or want. She wanted away from all of it. She felt so trapped and did not understand why she stayed. Her mind had been so messed with that she did not know up from down anymore.

So, on this hot summer day with the Princess away, she had found herself surrounded by the Beast and a group of his like-minded friends. She did not know if it was the heat, her total level of fed up, or a combination of everything, but she had been restless, and a rebelliousness was rearing up inside. The Beast had left her with his friends to either go buy drugs, alcohol, or both. She did not know which nor did she care anymore.

His friends were already drunk or high and being loud, boisterous idiots. Without saying a word to any of them, she grabbed her keys and slipped out, unnoticed. She should have went and gotten the Princess and ran away, but she had no place to run to. The situation with the Beast had alienated her from her family. The Queen, King, and Prince were all fed up with her "choices." The King and Prince had disowned her, and the Queen only spoke to her about the Princess. Beauty had no friends anymore. She had no one except the Princess, the Beast, and his loathsome family.

With no place to go, she just drove. Heading down the main street of the town, she found herself sitting in front of the very bar where the Beast had met his Bar-Wench. Deciding to see the scene of the crime for herself, she went inside and sat down at the bar. She had very little cash and just ordered water, when her phone rang. She looked at the caller ID. It was the Beast's best friend. She thought that odd. She did not even know he had her number. He acted like he hated her so Beauty never paid much attention to him. The Beast had caused Beauty to feel resentment toward his friend, because the Beast idolized the man. Ever since Beauty met the Beast, his best friend had been a thorn on Beauty's side. He was always going on and on about the friend's accomplishments. Beauty did not see what the big deal was. To her, the guy was very disrespectful and ungrateful for any kindness she showed him. He looked like he never took a bath, was extremely selfish, and a drug addict on top of everything. In Beauty's opinion, he was not a good friend at all. But the Beast thought the guy crapped gold and it irked Beauty to no end.

Still she answered the call. "Hello?"

The deep voice responded with, "Beauty?"

"Yes?" She could hear rustling and people talking. A lot of commotion. Was that yelling?

He cleared his throat, sounding very calm. Not at all boisterous like when she had left.

"Let me bend your ear for a minute. Well, you see... the Beast, he left here and is trying to find you. And well, you have a family locator on your phone. He was real upset and well... he lost control of his truck while he was peeling out of the parking lot. He hit a cop car and pushed it five spaces into a neighbor's car. Then, he kept going."

Beauty did not even know what to say. She became engulfed in fear, all she could croak out was, "Umm, ok, yeah." Before she hung up.

No sooner had Beauty stood and turned toward the door did the Beast come barreling into the bar with a look so killing her blood ran cold at the sight of him. She did not have time to say a word before he pounced on her, jerking her by the hair, and dragging her stumbling out the door. A roomful of people witnessed it all. He was dragging Beauty and screaming at her.

"Are you allowed to go out alone? Are you allowed to go to the bar? NO, YOU ARE NOT!"

As they reached the Beast's truck, she could see the damage, but still he continued to scream. The Beast was out of his mind.

"LOOK WHAT YOU MADE ME DO! MY HOOD WON'T STAY SHUT AND I HAD TO DRIVE THREE MILES DOWN THE ROAD

WITH MY HEAD OUT THE WINDOW LIKE ACE VENTURA!"

Blood was rushing into Beauty's head with the pain of his grip. Her words were low and frightened.

"I'm sorry, I'm sorry, I'm sorry," was all she could get to come out of her mouth.

People were starting to come out of the bar and stare. The Beast did not care. He took Beauty's cell phone from her hand and threw it against the concrete wall of the building the bar was located in. Then, he spit in her face and screamed, "GET IN THE TRUCK!"

She was trying to reason with him. To tell him they had an audience and to please stop hurting her where people could see. She tried to make him understand that she would be good. They could leave the truck since it was damaged, and she would drive them home, but the Beast was unreachable in his rage. He did not want to hear anything she had to say. Instead, he forced Beauty into the truck. He repeatedly slammed her head into the metal frame. Blood began to blur her vision and she was feeling dizzy. Like the wild Beast he was, the sight only made him more incensed. He began to strangle Beauty. She fought against his calloused hands wrapped around her tender throat, but she was no match for the Beast. Black spots began to dance before her eyes, and little star bursts flitted across her vision. All she could see was the Beast's face as her struggles began to become weaker. She thought of the Princess and prayed the Queen would get custody. Surely, when the Beast killed her in public, with witnesses, he would go to prison. At least then, the Princess would be free.

Beauty could feel herself dying. She did not even register that the Beast had pushed her onto the hot tar blacktop of the street where his truck was parked. It felt like time slowed as the world faded away. Then suddenly, the Beast's hands were gone, and Beauty was choking, gasping for breath. Through slitted eyes, she saw six big men fighting and trying to restrain the Beast, who was still trying to get to her. Weak in the knees and barely breathing, Beauty tried to stand. She needed to run. To flee. She needed to do something. But as she stood, her knees buckled, and she crumpled face first onto the pavement. She could still see the men fighting the Beast. Her eyes were locked on the free-for-all violence. There was such an awful ringing in her ears. Her head and throat ached. People were around her, kneeling next to her, speaking to her – but she could not respond. All she could do was stare at the Beast. The ringing grew more and more intense with each passing second, and it registered to Beauty that her ears were not ringing – she was hearing sirens. Unable to hold out any longer, she started to slip into darkness. Right before she did, she locked eyes with the Beast, and his menacing look of hatred was the last thing she saw before the blackness engulfed her.

14

A dream is a wish the heart makes... A nightmare is the remnant of a broken soul...

Chaos, total chaos. That was what Beauty was immersed in. She sat on the curb of one side of the street, surrounded by policemen, while the Beast sat handcuffed across the street directly in front of her. His rage had not ebbed. Between hateful glares and jabs at the police officers, the Beast screamed at Beauty.

"KEEP YOUR MOUTH SHUT, BITCH!"

"ARE YOU HAPPY NOW, BEAUTY?"

"LOOK WHAT YOU HAVE DONE, BITCH!"

"WHEN I GET OUT, YOU ARE GOING TO PAY!"

Beauty was in shock. She could barely understand the questions the police asked her. She numbly let the EMS examine her. The police took photos and had her sign a statement. She did not even read what was written for her. She was a mess of fear and shock. The police told her that the Beast would be charged with attempted murder, not just assault. It was against the rules where they lived to attempt to strangle someone. That was an automatic attempted murder charge. If the police only knew how many times the Beast had "attempted" to murder her behind closed doors, he would be facing many charges.

The sun had gone down by the time the police finally took the Beast away. The crowd had started to disburse when Beauty noticed the Wicked Bitch holding the Princess, watching everything. The police officer speaking with Beauty followed her gaze to the beautiful little girl and Wicked woman.

"Do you know them, Miss?"

Beauty was able to nod yes, and whisper, "That's his mother and my daughter."

The officer just shook his head and looked at Beauty with sympathy.

"What kind of person brings a child to witness this?"

The words were out of her mouth before she could stop them.

"The kind that spawns Satan."

The officer did not even bat an eye at Beauty's statement. He just nodded and told her,

"You are clear to go, Ma'am. If I were in your place, I would go get my child and get far away from these people."

Beauty nodded and thanked the officer as he handed her the almost undamaged cell phone an officer had retrieved from the concrete outside the bar. She approached the Wicked Woman and without a word, she took the Princess from her arms and turned to leave.

The Wicked Bitch's words did not even make Beauty slow her stride.

"He will get out, you know, and he will not be coming to stay with me. Prepare yourself."

Beauty just wanted to hold the Princess and go home. She felt no urge to cry or rage anymore. She just felt shame over all the witnesses. Shame that his vile mother brought the sweet, innocent Princess to witness such drama. She should not have been surprised. The Beast's apple did not fall far from the tree.

When Beauty arrived home, the house was quiet and dark. She was so thankful for the silence. The Princess was so young, but she looked at Beauty with big, hazel eyes, and Beauty could swear she saw sadness in them. The Princess brought one tiny hand to Beauty's bruised face and said, "Mamma hurt?"

Beauty felt the tears pricking her eyes. "No baby, Mamma not hurt. Mamma is ok. We are both ok. Everything is going to be ok."

The sweet Princess smiled at Beauty, and she felt a warmth in her chest. It was going to be ok. The Beast was gone and would be for a long time. They were going to move on and be free from the torture. At this realization, a calm began to set into Beauty. Hope sparked inside her. She had her daughter and she could support them both. Everything was going to be ok.

It had been a hellish day, full of horrific acts, but that night, in those moments with her daughter, Beauty felt a peace she had not known in a very long time. Her life had been so unstable for so long. She never knew from one day to the next what kind of terror the day would bring, but she knew now that tomorrow would be different. Tomorrow would be a new beginning for Beauty and the Princess.

In the darkness, the only sound was her baby girl's soft breaths as she slept.

Beauty rocked her daughter and felt relief.

15

I knew who I was this morning... But I have changed a few times since then

Beauty was awakened from her first sound sleep in ages by her ringing cell phone. It was three o'clock in the morning. Who would be calling at this awful hour? She did not recognize the number, so she did not answer. The phone ringing ended and then immediately started up again. Afraid the sound would wake the baby, she got out of bed and moved from the room quietly. By the time Beauty was shutting the door, the phone had stopped again, and started ringing again. She finally answered with a sleepy hello.

The voice on the other end of the phone made her stomach drop.

"Come bail me out."

Beauty could not even form words. She just stayed silent as her sleep-addled mind grasped at thoughts. How was this possible? How was he calling her? Didn't people have to accept collect calls from jail or something like that? The movies and TV shows always showed scenes where people had to accept collect calls. Isn't that how it really worked?

The impatient voice on the other end brought Beauty's brain crashing back to reality.

"I SAID COME BAIL ME OUT!"

Oh no, did he say bail? There was no way he got bail. He tried to kill her. Is the justice system that flawed?

Beauty acted out of fear. She hung up and immediately shut off the cell phone. Her brain racing with a million different terrifying thoughts. He will not get out! He cannot get out! None of his family will bail him out! Right? I mean, they have had to do that too many times before and he still owes them money.

A sick feeling began to rest like a lead

weight in the pit of Beauty's stomach. No, she thought with resolve. No, none of them will bail him out. I have nothing to be worried about. Beauty kept reassuring herself. Unable to sleep, she did menial tasks around the house until it was time to get ready for work. She had to do a stellar cover-up job with her make-up that morning. There was bruising around her left temple and significant bruising around her neck. The cuts and scrapes to her body were covered with a long-sleeved shirt and pants. She opted for a turtleneck even though it was going to be another hot summer day, but she could get away with it since it was always cold at work. If anyone asked about her eye, she would laugh it off and say she was such a klutz and walked into an open kitchen cabinet while half asleep. She felt confident in her stories and hoped no one would ask.

She stuck with her morning routine and got the Princess ready for the day. She dropped the Princess off with the babysitter and headed to work, all the while doing her best not to think about the Beast or the fact that he had gotten bail. She listened to chipper music at high volumes and sang along at the top of her lungs, but unwelcomed thoughts would still seep in. She

His friends were no real friends at all. His family valued money more than they valued each other and none of them really cared enough to help him. He would sit and rot in jail where he belonged. She and the Princess could be free to live a happy life without him. It was the start of a new chapter. Still, she could feel a niggling sense of fear. It was a tingling in her spine that would not go away. As she went through her day and robotically did her job, she smiled and pretended all was well. She never turned her cell phone back on.

She was just getting finished up for the day and telling all her co-workers goodbye as they headed out the back door of the building, when a sight made her blood run cold and stopped her in her tracks. She wanted to run back inside. She wanted to scream and vomit all at the same time. Instead, she just stood there motionless, watching the Beast leaning up against her car.

He wore the same clothes from the day before, with a large blood-crusted cut along his forehead on his hair line. Dried blood coated his blonde hair. There was bruising along his cheekbones and dark shadows below his cold, blue eyes. His clothes were a dirty mess of blood dirt, and God only knew what else. She could see the knuckles of both his hands were split in several places, with cuts and bruising.

Beauty was terrified and very embarrassed. She did not want any of her co-workers to notice him. He looked like a dirty lunatic that had escaped from the local psychiatric hospital. How had she ever thought this Beast was attractive? In that moment, there was none of the charm he imitated so well.

Her feet felt rooted to their spot on the concrete. They eyed each other. She could tell the Beast was taking her measure and preparing to chase her if she tried to run. She did not want a scene outside of her work. She needed her job.

Finally, with a slow exhalation of breath, Beauty took slow, tired steps toward the Beast and her car. The short distance across the parking lot felt like she was being escorted down the corridor of death row on her way to her execution. When she was finally within touching distance of the Beast, he crossed his arms over his chest and stared Beauty right in the eyes. She was so tired. She did not have the strength to do this. She did not want to fight anymore. Every time she began to feel hope, he would find a way to destroy it. That is what the Beast was. He was a destroyer of anything good.

Beauty could feel herself wilting under his gaze. She was retreating into herself and going into self-preservation mode. She ducked her head from his intense gaze and prayed he would not attack her and cost her the job she needed so badly.

The Beast reached out and brushed a stray strand of Beauty's raven hair from her cheek, inspecting her temple. He began to rub the make-up away until her bruise was more visible. Her body tensed at his touch, and the pain he caused against her tender flesh. His fingertips felt hot against her skin, still cold from the building she had just exited. He slowly glided them down her check to the top of her turtleneck. Beauty did not move. She did not even think she was breathing as he pulled down her collar and caressed the marks he left on her neck. Anxiety grew inside her. Her head shot up from staring at their feet and began to dart around, looking for anyone or any place of salvation from this monster. What if he had come to finish the job? He was being so calm and had been so still as she approached. What if he was in viper mode ready to strike? The Beast must have sensed Beauty's rising anxiety because he dropped his hands from her neck and placed one on each of her arms. His grip was firm but not painful. It was a silent statement not to run. She hated how he could anticipate her plans. He was like a damn mind reader.

She expected the Beast to lash out at any moment and kill her where she stood. The seconds that he held her in place felt like hours. Beauty could feel her heart beating so hard that she thought it was going to beat right out of her chest. The sound of it was thundering in her ears. Her breaths became pants and she could feel tears beginning to sting the corners of her eyes. Her body began to tremble uncontrollably, and she realized that she must be having a panic attack. She had felt symptoms before, but never this strong. She suddenly became extremely nauseated. She had not eaten all day but what little bit of liquids she had in her stomach were threatening to come up and spew out exorcist-style all over the Beast.

At that thought, Beauty began to laugh hysterically. Maybe she was having a nervous breakdown? The loss of all hope could do that to a person. Maybe her mind had completely snapped at the sight of the Beast roaming free.

Every time Beauty thought she knew what

the Beast would do next, he would pull a rabbit out of his bag of tricks and surprise her. Instead of being violent or killing her where she stood, he took her trembling body into his arms and caressed her back. His embrace was almost soothing and placating. He whispered soft words into her hair.

"Shhhh, it's ok. You are going to be ok."

"Shhhh, we're ok. We are going to be ok."

"Shhhh, I'm not mad. It happened. It's over. You will fix it."

Beauty let him do this as she sobbed. The parking lot was empty now except for her and the Beast, and she sobbed hysterically into her monster's arms. She could feel something vital inside her breaking. Pieces of herself breaking off. Pieces of her soul and the light inside her disintegrating into nothing. She could feel a darkness growing as her light was extinguished. Little by little, the Beast was taking from her and she was dying inside. Beauty cried for the loss. She cried until she only had the harsh silent sobs of breath escaping her gaping mouth. She ugly cried with all she had, until the blissful numbness she always felt after every breakdown began to set in. She had cried so much that at some point, her body went limp, and the Beast was all that was holding her up.

With silence and a blank expression, he escorted her to the passenger side of the car.

"Give me the keys."

With robotic movements, Beauty did as she was told, and the Beast buckled her into the seat. She stared blankly and said nothing as he started the car and drove to pick up the Princess. The Beast was all smiles as he got the little girl from her sitter. The Princess and the sitter both looked wary of the Beast, but then the Princess saw Beauty and cried, "Mama," with childlike glee. This seemed to placate the sitter and the Beast said his goodbyes to the woman.

As the Beast approached the car with the Princess in his arms, he was smiling and animated with the child; hugging, kissing, and tickling her. The little girl seemed delighted. Beauty watched through the glass of the windshield as the Princess touched the Beast's forehead. Her little face scrunched up into a baby scowl.

"Daddy hurt?"

The Beast chuckled softly to the girl.

"No, Daddy not hurt. Nothing can hurt daddy."

The sweet, little Princess seemed to accept this answer and patted his cheek with a tiny hand.

When the Beast went to put the Princess in the back seat, she insisted on a hug from Mommy. Her little arms were outstretched to Beauty and the smile on her lovely face melted some of the numbness Beauty felt inside. The Beast looked at Beauty through the open car door as she embraced the Princess, and all traces of the love he had been showing the child disappeared. When the Princess let go of Beauty and planted a sweet kiss on her cheek, the Beast scooped up the little girl in a flourish of playfulness and situated the girl in her car seat.

The giggles of the sweet Princess filled the car as the Beast started the ignition and looked over at Beauty. He lifted his hand toward her face and she flinched in response. A false smile spread across his face and a cold resolution glimmered in his eyes. His voice was overtly chipper as he caressed Beauty's cheek.

"Daddy is so happy to be going home with his girls."

Beauty wanted to gag.

16

When you can't look on the bright side, I will sit with you in the dark...

The Beast went into honeymoon mode. They never spoke of the actual "incident" but Beauty did inquire about how he had made bail. The Beast told her his father had helped and he had given the bail bondsman the title to his truck. He thought it was hilarious, because the bondsman had no clue the truck was totaled.

The Beast spent the next few months holding his

temper at bay. He acted remorseful for his actions and tried to slip back into his "boy" persona. Beauty knew it was all a lie, the Boy did not exist. Because of the Beast's actions that day, Beauty got kicked out of her home. The gated community had a clause that no one living on the property or visiting anyone on the property could commit an arrestable offense on the property grounds. So, for the first time, Beauty was evicted from her home.

The Beast's loathsome best friend came to the rescue like the superhero Beast idolized him to be. The friend lived in a duplex and the apartment right next to his had been available. With a good word from him, Beauty, the Beast, and the Princess, moved into the duplex. It was run down, in a shady part of town, and a far cry from any place Beauty had ever lived. She did not feel safe inside her home or outside of it. The Beast was overjoyed. He loved it and thought the place was perfect.

"But of course, he would," Beauty thought. His sleazy friend was right next door.

Beauty lived her life day by day and with each passing day, the Beast's ability to keep his temper in check waned. He pretended to fear nothing, but in reality, he feared the loss of his freedom very much. He had serious charges looming over his head and he expected Beauty to do everything she could to stop him from losing his freedom. He wrote a statement contradicting the one she had given at the scene. The statement was so absurd it basically contradicted the statement of every witness, but the Beast did not care. He made Beauty sign it anyway. The Beast's lawyer advised him that Beauty had to attend a class explaining what domestic abuse was, then sign a legal statement that she was not in any way abused. Her class certificates and statements were presented to the courts to get the charges against the Beast dropped. The Beast believed that Beauty could get the charges dropped if she requested that no charges be brought against him. He was ignorant and wrong.

Beauty learned that the Beast already had two Family Violence charges on his record, which happened on the same month he met Beauty. She also found out that in the State they lived in, the State could choose to pursue charges, even if she asked them not to. That fact, combined with his previous Family Violence charges, meant the State would go through with the case. The Beast was livid with Beauty and started to go back to his abusive ways.

In a matter of one summer, Beauty had moved twice, and started a new job. Separated from the Beast and thinking she was free. She was then forced back into his clutches through acts of rape and violence. Almost killed by the Beast and forced to jump through hoops and lies to try and make his court case go away. She was barely holding it together. Daily life was a blur. Only the fights, violence, and rape stuck out in her mind. She did not know how she managed to make it through each day at work and pretend to be normal, but she had to work. She even picked up more hours because the Beast had quit his job. His drug use had increased, and his erratic behavior made it impossible for him to hold down any kind of job.

He was spending all their money on drugs, and no bills were being paid. They were being evicted again and Beauty's car got repossessed. She had never been so low in her life. The Beast was not only using Beauty to please his every sadistic need, but now, he was turning her into a repulsive person. One who owed people money and lied. Her word was no good. All promises she made to pay were false promises, because the Beast blew through all the money the minute it hit the account.

Beauty had become someone she never thought she would be. Her whole life, she had strived for wonderful things, and now, she could not even keep a roof over her head or a car to drive.

The Queen stepped in and helped Beauty get another vehicle. Beauty took all her money from her next paycheck and found them a nice house in a nice neighborhood, and they moved in the darkness of night. She hated the way these actions made her feel like a thief slipping out into the night. But what choice did she have? The Beast was her burden and she had to keep a home, vehicle, and food for the Princess.

Beauty got very lucky with the new home. It was a beautiful, large mansion compared to the shady little duplex. A two-story new construction with a large backyard and a safe neighborhood. The Beast even seemed proud of it and tried to get his act together some. Getting him away from his druggie friend next door curbed some of the drug use and the Beast was able to get a job. A decent job, to Beauty's surprise. He made good money and they finally seemed to be on track to being financially stable.

However, the Beast was a destroyer. The more stable life became, the harder it became for him to keep his temper in check. His violent rages were weekly, not daily. Most likely because he did not have controlled substances in his system to provoke them. His drug of choice was mostly pot and he became sedated until his mental issues would overtake him, and he would lash out at Beauty. She learned in the first few months that being thrown down a high flight of stairs was very painful, and she swore she would never again live in a two-story house.

As the air grew cooler and fall settled in Beauty began to be sick. She was standing in a fast-food restaurant with the Beast and his family when she rushed out of line and into the bathroom. The Drama Queen followed her in and listened as Beauty retched up all the contents of her stomach. She thought for sure she had a stomach flu or food poisoning. As she washed her face and gargled with water, she looked up to see the Drama Queen staring at her, a smirk on her lips.

"Are you sure that is the problem?"

Beauty was perplexed

"What do you mean?"

The Drama Queen approached Beauty and rummaged around in her huge purse. With an aha look, she pulled out a white stick and handed it to Beauty.

"What I mean is maybe you should go take this."

Beauty raised an eyebrow. "You carry pregnancy tests around in your purse?"

The Drama Queen just shrugged and shooed Beauty into a stall. With her vile sister in-law hovering just outside the dented metal door of the stall, Beauty peed on the stick. And waited…and waited…praying for a negative. Instead, two pink lines formed, and her heart sank. She was not unhappy to have a child growing inside her. She was unhappy to have his child inside her. How could she have been so stupid? How could she have let this happen? She was on birth control. She took it faithfully even though she kept it hidden and the Beast did not know. He did not want her on birth control. He wanted more children, but she had almost died during the first pregnancy. Beauty tried to remember the last time she had her period. It had been at least two months ago. Maybe more. She had thought it was from stress and she bled sometimes after the rapes, so she couldn't tell what was her cycle and what was from trauma. When she was on birth control, the cycles never lasted more than two days and she showed very few symptoms. So, she thought, maybe all the stress had caused her to be lighter or not have her period at all.

She was such an idiot, and this was her life. Another momentous change and it was happening in a fast food restaurant stall, with her sitting on a toilet, freaking out. The Drama Queen's shrill voice brought Beauty back to reality.

"So, what's it say? I've been waiting out here ten minutes."

All Beauty could do was unlock the stall, step out, and hand the Drama Queen the stick. The woman went nuts with joy. She was jumping up and down, acting so excited like she was the one pregnant. She even pocked the positive pregnancy test.

Beauty thought, "Huh, I wonder if she's going to hold on to that to try and trap some guy into thinking she's pregnant and marrying her. Then, faking a miscarriage. I could totally see this Bitch doing that."

The Drama Queen continued to be overjoyed and Beauty just stared. A knock came at the bathroom door, followed by the Beast's deep voice.

"Everything ok in there? You better not be doing anything kinky with my beautiful wife!"

The Drama Queen pulled the stick from her purse and announced loud enough for everyone in the whole fast food restaurant to hear.

"She's pregnant! Beauty's pregnant!"

Beauty's face turned beet red. She was in white-trash hell and this bitch had no shame. The Beast's gaze was intense.

"Is it true?"

Beauty nodded and pointed at her bouncing she-devil of a sister in-law. "According to the stick she carries around in her purse."

A slow smile spread across the Beast's face as he eyed her belly. It made Beauty uneasy and her first thought was, "Oh God, please don't let it be a boy!"

17

It would be so nice if something would make sense for a change...

L ife had a funny way of jumping up and biting Beauty in the butt. After months, hell, even years of instability, she had managed to find a home, keep a job, and hold her sanity together throughout all the chaos. And then, she finds herself pregnant. With no health insurance, yet.

When they had returned home on the night she found out about the pregnancy, Beauty put the sweet princess to bed and walked wearily toward the living room. The Beast sat on one of the antique sofas and patted the seat next to him. She sat down, and her head fell back as a long sigh escaped her lips. The Beast was quiet for a long time. His faced looked pensive, as if he were deep in thought. Beauty was nearly asleep when he finally spoke.

"This time it will be a boy and things are going to be different."

Beauty just sat quietly, stunned. The Beast had done another unimaginable thing. He had slid from the couch and was kneeling in front of her. His body seemed tense as he started to proclaim that this pregnancy would be different. He made her promises of a better life. Promised no more torture. Promised he would be a good man. Promises of no more drugs. Promised he wanted to be a man and not a monster. Promises, promises, promises. Beauty had heard his promises so many times that her only response was, "Actions speak louder than words. Of all the many cruel lessons you have taught me, I know this one well. If someone is truly sorry for what they have done to you, the best way they can show their remorse is not to repeat that action."

At her statement, with his rough hands clasped around her small ones, the Beast regarded Beauty with a look she could almost believe was admiration. Not love, no, the Beast did not know what love was. His version of it meant pain. He thought love had to hurt and that the only way to show love was through pain or pushing the other person to the brink of insanity. His logic was one Beauty thought she would never understand, but in that moment, as he gave her that look, the puzzle pieces that had never quite fit started to come together. He looked almost vulnerable. Beauty had regarded her situation as a dangerous chess match where everyone and every aspect of their lives played into the ongoing brutal game. She thought the Beast viewed her as a pawn to his King, but Beauty was quickly beginning to realize that she was the Queen to his King, and in chess, the Queen is the most important piece on the board. The King is nothing without the Queen, and to the Beast, she was his Queen. It was a game changer.

Beauty looked at the Beast. Really looked at the monster in front of her. She tried to see the man, not the monster. She took in his gaunt appearance, disheveled clothes and pleading eyes. Beauty had spent so much time fearing this Beast and feeling like nothing to him, yet looking at him now, she saw she was everything. In a very sadistic, messed up way, she was everything to the Beast, and the thought unnerved her.

Beauty was the only thing holding him together. Without her, he would spiral out of control and she did not want that responsibility. He had twisted her mind so thoroughly that she felt pity for her monster, maybe even a real love, not the false one she had been playing at.

He was like Frankenstein's monster, a creation of sadistic parents who showed no love and had left him to fend for himself with no concept of what love was.

Beauty had been asking herself for years why she had put up with his torments and degradations, and she realized that somewhere deep down in her dwindling soul, she thought she could change the Beast. The will to stay had been born out of fear, but somewhere along this journey, it had morphed into something much more complicated. Beauty was trying to teach this monster what real love was. In doing so, she had given almost every part of herself and taken all the brutality and pain he dished out to try and teach him he was worthy of love. He had been killing pieces of her, and she had been allowing it.

Beauty felt like her life was so complicated and extremely simple all at the same time. The fact was, she could not change the Beast. No amount of love can make a monster into a man, but she had held on to that glimmer of hope.

Before she met the Beast, her life had been black and white. Beauty knew right from wrong. She knew good and bad. Now, her life was so many different shades of gray that she could not even see black or white anymore.

The Beast wanted Beauty to make him her entire world and would lash out whenever he felt her attention was not solely on him. That was a precarious position to be in, because one person could not be your entire world. She had a daughter that was her world. She had to have a job and she loved her family, but the Beast understood none of that. He was like a child in so many ways. A brutal, selfish, violent child that lashed out at Beauty whenever he did not get his way. How was she supposed to please the Beast, especially with another child on the way? He was already so jealous of the Princess.

Her head spun with many thoughts. So many pieces of the never-ending puzzle she was stuck in. She wanted to crawl under a rock and hide from the world. That was Beauty's way –

she was an avoider. If she could not deal with a situation, she withdrew inside herself and blocked out whatever was going on. That was how she had dealt with the Beast's tortures and that was how she was dealing with this unexpected side of the Beast now.

She did not want to feel sympathy or try to fix him anymore. She wanted to take the Princess and run far away. Beauty did not want her life and she feared that she did not want the baby growing inside her. She wanted to pretend it did not exist. Her feelings of disgust over these thoughts overwhelmed her. None of this was the fault of the little Prince or Princess growing inside her, but she could not help feeling the way she did. When the Princess was growing in her belly, Beauty had felt joy and love. She wanted to protect her baby, but now, after everything she had been through, she feared there was no love inside her for another little person.

With a weary sigh, Beauty looked at the Beast and whispered, "I'm going to bed."

He smiled and nodded. He followed her but did not make any sexual advances. He did not act angry or expectant of anything. The Beast was gentle and kind, helping Beauty change into her night clothes and even tucking her in with a kiss to her forehead. When he came to bed, he slid in close to her and wrapped his arms around her in a loving way. His voice a deep low whisper in her ear.

"I love you. I promise, this time will be different."

A lone tear slid down Beauty's cheek. It was tender moments like this one that hurt her the most because they were the ones that stoked that fire of hope inside her... and she did not want to feel hope. As far as the Beast was concerned, Beauty wanted to feel nothing for him ever again.

18

**Be careful what you wish for,
you just might get it...**

For two months, the Beast made good on his promises, but this did not make Beauty happy. It made her very uneasy. She was constantly on edge, waiting for him to slip and go into a rage, but he didn't. Instead, he went to work, paid attention to the Princess, stayed off the hard drugs, and was attentive to Beauty.

Beauty felt her life was in that calm before the storm. It was like those moments right before the edges of a hurricane made land fall. The wind was nonexistent, and everything was eerily quiet, but you knew something bad was coming. Something that could possibly be catastrophic and life changing. Beauty lived every day for two months with that feeling growing inside her.

Fall arrived, and the leaves turned brown and fell away from the trees. The signs of a southern winter showing, with each day that neared the holiday season. Those were cold and rainy days where Beauty would stare out the window and revert inside herself, just watching and listening to the rain fall. The tenderness the Beast had shown her caused Beauty to burrow deeper into the chaos of her mind. She did not know how to react to a tender touch or tender emotions from a man. She reacted to her daughter, but it was beginning to feel forced. She loved the Princess more than life itself, but Beauty was quickly becoming detached from the world.

The pregnancy was ever present in Beauty's mind. She had calculated that the baby would be due sometime early in the summer. When her health insurance finally became valid, Beauty made her first doctor's appointment. She was already way behind on them and nearing her second trimester. The day came for her first appointment and Beauty got a blood test. The Doctor confirmed her pregnancy and sent her for an ultrasound.

The ultrasound tech was a sweet, round woman, all bubbles and cheer as Beauty prepared for the test. They made small talk as the woman glided the cold wand across her belly. Beauty waited for the heartbeat. She waited for the tech to turn the screen and show her the little bean in her belly... but none of that happened. She saw the exact moment the woman's face shut down into a mask of professional indifference.

"Is something wrong? Is the baby ok?" Beauty heard the panic rising in her voice. "Please, let me see the baby. Is everything ok?"

The ultrasound tech looked at her and Beauty could see the pity in her eyes as she spoke.

"I need you to get cleaned up and go take a set in the emergency room lobby. The Doctor will be with you shortly to speak with you."

Beauty felt a sense of dread and that old familiar numbness.

"Ok."

As she cleaned up the cold gel from her skin, dressed and headed to the ER waiting room, Beauty was in a daze. But her feet moved, and she made it to her destination. She sat quietly, waiting for the Doctor for what felt like hours. When he finally approached her, Beauty was on the verge of panic.

"What's wrong with my baby?"

The Doctor sat down with her, his voice trying to be calm and soothing.

"The fetus is in your tube."

Beauty nodded. "Ok, what does that mean? Can we move it with surgery?"

The Doctors eyes looked so sad.

"No, honey, even if that was possible, there is no heartbeat. The fetus is not alive. In fact, it has not been alive for some time. You should be going into your second trimester and the measurements show it lived to be about nine weeks. You are actually very lucky. Had the fetus not died and continued to grow, your tube would have ruptured, and your life could have been lost as well."

Beauty felt bile rising in her throat. This was her fault. She had not felt love for the child or warmed to the thought of it. She had been living in a darkness for two months pretending it did not exist and it had died inside of her. She did vomit then. All over the floor. She had a dead baby inside her and had been walking around with it inside her for two months. God or karma or whatever was out in the universe had to be punishing her.

When the retching was done, the tears came. She cried for the baby she should have embraced and loved. She cried for the pitiful excuse of a person she had become. She cried because that was all she could do at that moment.

Someone from the hospital had called the Beast. He had arrived and was still being the tender version of his monstrous self. He kept whispering to her that it would be alright. They would try again. He was not disappointed in her failure.

At some point, the Doctors had admitted her into the ER and had given her something to calm her down. They explained that they had to administer a drug to break up the fetus, so she could then pass it as a miscarriage. Then, her blood levels would be monitored and if need be, a DNC would be performed to remove any parts of the fetus left behind.

Everything the Doctors said passed through one ear and out the other. Whatever the Doctors had given her made her world comfortably quiet and numb. She lay on the hospital bed drifting in and out of consciousness. She vaguely recalled a nurse telling her that they were administering the drug to force a miscarriage. Beauty did not know how long after they gave her the drug that the pain started, but when it did, it was like white hot pokers being jabbed into her abdomen and pelvis. She awoke from unconsciousness and cried out in pain. The nurses were instantly beside her, administering more drugs. These drugs were for the pain and within seconds, the pain had subsided, and Beauty felt like she was floating. She liked the feeling. She wanted to stay in that out-of-body floating feeling forever. It was nice in that place. There was no pain, no worries, no thoughts, no Beast. Just Beauty, floating and free.

Once, when she woke from the pain, she felt wetness all around her. When she lifted the sheet and her gown, there was blood. So much blood. Dark chunks of meat mixed with bright red pools and it was coming out of her. She felt sick at the sight and became hysterical. She could feel the Beast at her side, but she would not look at him. The nurse came in and gave her more drugs in her IV. Something to calm her and help with the pain. Beauty quickly forgot her worries and floated away to that happy numb place.

She stayed in the hospital all night. Everything was like a horrible nightmare mixed with bouts of euphoria.

When Beauty opened her eyes the next morning, she had a dull ache in her abdomen, but that was all. Her baby was gone.

She wanted to go home and forget all of it. The Beast was staring at her, looking tired and devoid of emotion.

Beauty's throat felt scratchy.

"I want to go home."

The Beast nodded and left the room. Beauty lay there, not wanting to move. She felt dirty and hung over from all the drugs. The Beast returned with a nurse and he signed the release papers for Beauty, after she gave her instructions and prescriptions. Beauty was to go home and rest for at least three days. She was to take her pain medication and if she had any complications, to come back to the hospital. Beauty thanked the nurse as she left. The Beast was very quiet as he helped her dress. They were both quiet. The ride home was quiet. The house was eerily quiet as they stepped inside.

"Where is the Princess?"

"Your mother took her to her house for the night."

Beauty nodded and padded slowly toward the couch and slumped on it, staring blankly into space. Her eyelids felt heavy. Even though she had slept on and off throughout the night, she felt a bone-deep exhaustion. Her body could not stay awake... it needed to rest and heal.

Beauty was surprised when the Beast lifted her head and placed a pillow beneath it. He then covered her with a blanket and placed his hand on her hip as he sat down beside her.

The blue glow of the TV illuminated his profile as he turned it on and began to flip through channels. Beauty's last thought before she drifted into the darkness of sleep was, "He is still being tender."

This surprised her. She was no longer pregnant. Didn't that mean the Beast had no motive for things to be different?"

19

Take Snow White out into the woods and kill her. As proof that she is dead, bring me her heart...

Beauty awoke the next morning to a house so silent you could have heard a pin drop. The Princess was still with the Queen and to her surprise, the Beast had gone to work. She lay awake for a very long time just watching the shadows dance across the ceiling. Her cell phone rested on the wooden coffee table beside the couch, a message light blinking green. A groan escaped her lips. Every muscle in her body ached as she reached for it. She could feel an ever present dull ache in her abdomen. She opened the message app.

The Beast: Good morning, beautiful. I made it to work. I hope you're feeling better. I love and miss you to the moon and back!

Beauty: Thank you. Glad you made it ok. I hope you have a wonderful day. I love you to the moon and back to.

Beauty was perplexed by the Beast's show of affection, especially since she had lost the baby. Texts messages were nothing new. He always told her he loved her. It was part of the game. If he did not tell her and withheld his affections, it was merely a tactic to make her worry that she had done something wrong and he was upset. Which would ultimately result in a fight and violence.

Beauty was like a wounded animal. Normally, the Beast would pounce on her when she was ill and weak. His favorite time to rape her was if she had fever because in his words, "She felt burning hot.".

Another text message popped up on her phone.

The Beast: I love you more! I miss you!

Beauty: I miss you too.

Beauty did not know how to reply to his

messages. She was confused and trying to figure out when the shoe was going to drop. Was he buttering her up to make her breakdown more enjoyable? Could he possibly feel any kind of real love or empathy for Beauty? No, she did not think it was possible.

Early in the relationship, she had noticed that when people told him something sad or painful, the Beast would merely nod.

She asked him, "Why don't you say you're sorry?"

His response was, "Why would I be sorry? It's not my fault."

Beauty explained to the Beast that it was the polite thing to do to show empathy or even sympathy when people shared their problems. Especially if they were a friend or family member that you're supposed to care about. It shows that you care. Beauty will never forget the look on Beast's face. It had been a combination of perplexed and calculating, like the thought had never occurred to him. But now that it had, he could use it to his advantage.

Beast had smiled. "So, all I have to do is say I'm sorry after someone tells me their sob story or problems and they will think I give a shit? Huh, I'll have to try it."

And he had tried it. Many times, Beauty had watched as he perfected another facet of his many false faces. She hated that she had helped add to his arsenal of manipulation.

Her phone blinked with another message.

The Beast: I'm sorry you are hurting.

Beauty: Thank you.

There was the manipulation with his false empathy. He almost had her believing he cared, but she knew he really didn't. The Beast had no real empathy or sympathy. His only true emotions were his rage and his pleasure. Everything else was whatever manifestation he thought would bring about the outcome he wanted. Every situation in his game had an emotion to fit it and the Beast thought he was a master. Beauty knew he wasn't. Whatever he was playing at now, she would figure it out. She had noticed the cracks. The Beast was unraveling. With each passing day he attempted to walk the line, his dark needs rose a little closer to the surface.

Beauty may be at home recovering from her miscarriage, but the break gave her time to think and plan. She had time to prepare herself for the next screw-up. It was inevitable. The Beast would finally snap, unable to keep his demons at bay, and he would go back to drugs and the abuse. They were his addictions, just like her pain.

Her message light blinked.

The Beast: What is my Beauty doing?

Beauty thought, *preparing for your eventual fuck ups*. But what she texted was not that.

Beauty: Just resting.

A message immediately came through.

The Beast: My beautiful girl needs her rest to heal, and when the time is right, we will

try again.

Beauty: Ok.

Try again? Beauty would ask if he was serious, but why waste her breath or time? She knew he was very serious. The Beast did not care about the baby that they lost. All he cared about was the next one he could get into her. The Beast wanted a son. A little Beast to teach and twist into a mini version of him. A fourth-generation abuser with good looks and a sadistic personality.

The thought made Beauty sick to her stomach. She ran to the nearest bathroom and dry-heaved until her throat hurt.

20

There are far better things ahead than any we leave behind...

The holidays came and went with no outbursts or violence from the Beast. A new year passed with the Beast staying in and spending it with "his girls." Life had become strange; it was low-key, and major drama-free. Beauty adapted. If she had learned anything from her time with the Beast, she had learned how to quickly adapt. So, she took his new approach with a grain of salt. Beauty would adapt, but she would also keep her guard up.

The Beast had implemented a new normal.

She worked, and he worked. They spent evenings with the Princess and played at a normal life. Every day became mundane, and for a time, the Beast held fast to his promises. There were no major fights, no violence, no brutality. Just anxiety. Beauty was always on edge.

Days turned into a month. A month turned into a few months. The passing of time did nothing to ease Beauty's anticipation of the Beast's mental decline. She lived with the knowledge that he would break and revert to his old ways. The catalyst for this transformation could be something small or another life changing event.

Beauty had learned that the Beast was incapable of change. He was only capable of holding the demons at bay for longer periods of time. She lay awake at night wondering what had prompted his change, but she could not pinpoint one event other than her pregnancy. Which was now over. The uncertainty became too much to bear at times. Always waiting for the bogeyman to jump out and frighten her. It was an awful way to live.

Finally, as winter ended, and Spring began to blossom, Beauty got a reason for the Beast's good behavior.

It was the day the Beast had to make his final court appearance for the charges he was facing. The Beast made Beauty go with him to every court appearance. He thought it was imperative that they show a united front, and that she stand by his side like the supportive, good, little wife she pretended to be. Pretending had become second nature to Beauty. Her whole life was pretend.

The Beast's ongoing legal trouble from his attempt to kill Beauty in public had resulted in a third-degree Felony Domestic Violence charge and an offer of probation. The Beast would only see jail time if he broke any of his probation requirements. All of Beauty's forced efforts and the work of his lawyer had paid off. The Beast was free, but Beauty felt that the justice system had failed her. She had been forced to write statements and take that class. The prosecutors knew this, that is why they still pursued charges against the Beast. But more than their failures, Beauty failed herself and the Princess.

On that day, Beauty had to ask herself if the Beast's sadistic tendencies were rubbing off on her. It was an incident on the way to the courthouse that made her question what kind of person she was becoming. If finding pleasure in his humiliations was her, becoming twisted and sadistic like him, or merely a reaction from for all she'd been through.

They were driving to the courthouse dressed to impress. The Beast wore a nice, fitted, button-down shirt with khaki pants. Beauty was in a gray, understated, but elegant dress and heels. They looked like a beautiful young couple headed to church or about to have a meal at a nice restaurant. Anything to do with the judicial system made the Beast nervous. Beauty believed his only true fear was prison.

They had stopped at a light when he turned to her and said, "Oh no, I need baby wipes!"

Beauty stammered out, "W--what?"

The Beast's eyes were as large as saucers and his skin was a pasty color. She was so stunned at the way he looked that she did not register the smell. Then she realized why the Beast looked so distraught.

His voice was almost a shrill whine in the small enclosed car. "Baby Wipes, DAMN IT! I need them. I SHIT MY PANTS!"

It took everything in Beauty not to laugh. She plastered on a mask of indifference and dug around in the back seat until she found the baby wipes she always carried with her. When she presented them to the Beast, he attempted to drive while cleaning himself up. Beauty suggested he wait until they reached the court house and he listened to her suggestion.

She rolled down her window and turned her face into the morning sun, still trying not to smile. The Beast said nothing. His face was a mask of concentration.

"After all the shit this monster has put me through, it serves him right to have to sit in his own shit." The thought was fleeting, but it took her aback. When had she become so vindictive?

They finally pulled into the courthouse parking lot and the Beast resumed his cleaning. He took off his pants and boxers right there in the car. Beauty did not know where to look. She had seen this monster naked a thousand times, but at that moment, covered in his own feces, she wasn't sure if she was supposed to watch or not. He had witnessed her degradation so many times. He had been the one to inflict it and find pleasure in it. If Beauty did the same to him, did that make her a Beast as well?

The boxers were a lost cause and the Beast just threw them out the window. He cleaned himself and his pants the best he could. By the

157

time he was done, all the baby wipes were gone, and the car smelled like a dirty diaper. The Beast had muttered curses throughout the whole ordeal. At one point, he had looked up, and the expression on Beauty's face must have enraged him because he shot her one of his killing looks. She had turned away.

When they finally emerged from the vehicle, the Beast had to untuck his shirt to try and cover the big stain at the back of his khaki pants. Beauty was going to mention that his shirt had a mess on it as well, but the Beast growled a low, "Shut the FUCK UP!" in her direction.

So, Beauty did exactly as she was told, and let the Beast walk into the courthouse with his own shit visible all over the bottom of his shirt.

Beauty would have suggested the Beast go to the bathroom to check himself, but she had been told to stay quiet. When people visibly shrank away and did not sit next to them, Beauty acted as if she smelt nothing and kept her mouth shut. When the lawyers furrowed their brows and wrinkled theirs noses as they talked to the Beast, Beauty stayed stone-faced with her mouth shut. When the time came, and the Beast had to stand before the judge and accept his sentence in front of a courtroom of hundreds, the viable shit had dried and crusted to his back. Beauty said nothing. She did not laugh although she could hear others snickering. She did not show a single bit of emotion until the Beast turned from the permanently scowling judge.

Beauty watched the judge as the Beast talked to his lawyer. She saw the moment the judge noticed the shit and the stain. The judge's mask cracked, and he had to hold up a folder in front of his face and turn away from the microphone. When he turned back, with his mask in place, and scanned the crowd, his eyes stopped on Beauty. For a single second, she let the corners of her lips tip up in a smile. The judge did the same with a nod of acknowledgement.

Beauty laughed inside at the Beast's humiliation, but he never knew. By the time he had reached her and motioned for her to follow him out, Beauty's own mask was back in place.

That day, Beauty realized two important things. She did find a pleasure in his pain, and the promises he made were not for her. They were for himself. The Beast's good behavior was not because of any remorse he felt for his actions. It was because he could not risk getting in trouble again. He had to tamp down his demons or risk jail.

Beauty would be counting the days, wondering just how long the Beast could hold it together.

21

Would you like an adventure now or shall we have our tea first?

Beauty thought she would never get the smell out of her car, but eventually, it faded. Just like the happiness she felt over the Beast's public humiliation. She lived her life with a monster who had tried to kill her. She had kept the truth silent and regurgitated his lies like they were her own truth. Beauty felt she deserved his freedom and all the misery it would bring with it. Her rapist, attempted murderer, and stealer of her soul was the monster she chose to be with. Beauty had no self-worth left and the Beast's self-imposed good behavior began to unravel before the first three-digit heats of summer.

The first indication of coming change was missing money. The Beast was back on drugs. At first, Beauty tried to ignore the financial discrepancies. The Beast was not acting violent, but he was growing distant and when he was home, he was a walking, talking zombie. This time, he was obviously into a mellow drug and she preferred a subdued Beast to a violent one. Then, it all went to shit again. The Beast lost his job and all of Beauty's money went to hi drug use. The bills did not get paid and after a year in their big house, they were evicted again.

Beauty had to scramble to find a cheaper home. She found a broken down mobile home in the middle of nowhere. It was isolated, which the Beast loved. The location made Beauty very nervous, but she could not allow the Princess to be homeless. So, once again they moved.

They were in a shack surrounded by woods. The Beast was jobless and had too much time to fall deeper into a metal spiral fueled by drugs. This was a dangerous combination for Beauty. She was far from work and had to get up very early to get there on time. One morning, as she was about to leave for work, the Beast was sitting on the front porch. He was in the corner, his face hidden in shadows, and she did not see him at first. She almost jumped out of her skin when he spoke, and his tone made the hairs on the back of her neck prickle with alarm.

"Where are you going?"

"To work."

"I need money."

She backed away slowly, toward the steps of the rickety old porch.

"All I have is gas money."

The Beast said nothing, and Beauty took that as a cue that it was ok to leave. All she wanted to do was leave as quickly as she could.

She was carrying a still sleeping Princess in her arms as she descended the steps of the porch and unlocked her vehicle. She then buckled the Princess in and walked around the driver's side. She never heard him coming. With the door half ajar and while in the middle of placing her purse in the vehicle, she felt the gun barrel at her temple. Beauty froze, her only thought was, "Oh God, this is how I die. Please God, let the Princess not see."

The monster's voice was low and menacing.

"I said I need money, Bitch."

Beauty tried not to move. This was the first

time the Beast had pulled a gun on her. She had made it a point not to keep guns in the house for this very reason. Where had he gotten a rifle?

Her words were whispered and calm.

"I told you, all I have is gas money. I need it to get to and from work. If I do not work, there is no more money. I am sorry."

The Beast's response was to push the barrel harder into Beauty's temple making her wince in pain and stumble. She caught herself and leaned against the door, and the Beast moved closer to place the barrel under her chin. Beauty could feel tears stinging her eyelids. The fear inside her growing with every passing second. In the dancing shadows of the early morning light, his face looked distorted and grotesque as he moved closer to her.

"I don't care what you need the money for. You give it to me right now or I blow off your head, then mine, and leave that little girl with no parents."

For a fleeting moment, Beauty thought maybe, she should just let him do it. Maybe then the Princess would be better off without her troubled parents. Maybe it was the only way her baby could be free.

It was the first time since the baby's birth

that Beauty had considered death as an option. She was tired and weary of life. Her struggles were more than she could bear.

A moment passed between Beauty and her Beast. He knew she was weighing her options and pressed the barrel even harder into her chin. She relented and reached for purse.

"Just take it," she spat as she threw the money at him.

The Beast eyed her and then spit in her face as he pulled the gun back. Beauty flinched but held her ground. The Beast snatched the money from the ground and walked away. With his saliva dripping down her face, she got into her vehicle. Her hands shook as she held the wheel. She had not even wiped her face and could feel the tears coming. She was determined not to cry, until she looked in the rearview mirror and saw the Princess's beautiful, hazel eyes staring at her. A single tear slipped down Beauty's face as the realization hit her that the Princess had witnessed all of it. She hoped the little girl had just woken up. She prayed the baby had not seen.

As she pulled into the Queen's driveway and pulled the Princess from her car seat, the little girl used her blanket to wipe Beauty's face.

Beauty stared at her little girl. So tiny and small but her eyes, they looked wise beyond her years. Beauty hugged the little girl close and the Princess gripped her tightly.

"Mama ok," came the sweet little voice in Beauty's ear.

The tears flowed then.

"Yes, Baby. Mama ok."

The Princess's soft hair tickled Beauty's nose, but she did not care. All she wanted at that moment was to hold her baby and take comfort from the love she freely gave her. Innocent love. She wanted another life with her little girl. She wanted a life free of the Beast. She worried about the damage his actions were doing to the Princess and felt like the worst mother in the world. She vowed that no matter what, for her child, she would get free. Even if that meant she had to sacrifice herself to make sure the baby would live a life free of the Beast.

Beauty wiped her face and walked up the sidewalk to her mother's house. As she handed the Princess to the Queen, they both gave Beauty a sad look. The Queen's voice was low and menacing.

"What did the Son of a Bitch do now?"

Beauty just shook her head and backed

away.

"I'm fine, Mama. Everything is going to be ok."

Beauty left the Queen and the Princess standing in the doorway. As she drove away, she started to plan. If anything happened to her she would make sure the Princess was safe.

When Beauty got to work, she wrote out a document detailing the kinds of abuse she had endured. Then, composed another document stating that in case of her death, the Queen was to have full legal custody of the Princess. Beauty was embarrassed to admit all that she endured, but the documents needed to be legal, so she found a kind lady at work who was a notary and had the documents notarized. Beauty then placed the documents in a large envelope and sealed it. That evening, when she picked up the Princess, she gave the documents to her mother and told her.

"This is only to be opened if something happens to me."

The Queen was not happy. She had a million questions and things to say to Beauty.

"I know he hurts you."

Beauty cast her eyes low. She was too

ashamed to look at her strong, beautiful mother.

"How do you know that, Mama?"

"Because the baby has been saying Daddy hurts mommy, since she started talking. She told me Daddy push Mommy down stairs. Daddy punch Mommy. Daddy punch holes in the wall. Today, she said Daddy put gun to Mommy head. You're not safe. You must leave him. Stay here with me. Don't go home."

Beauty just shook her head. The Queen would never understand. The Beast would always find her. If she stayed with her mother, he would kill her too. Beauty could not put her at risk like that. The Queen was livid as Beauty quietly walked out the door. What could she say? There was nothing to say. Her Mother's voice echoed out to the car.

"What is wrong with you? He is a piece of shit and I raised you better. If you go back to him, then you deserve whatever he does to you."

Beauty knew her mother was only saying those things in anger. She knew if the Queen knew the extent of what the Beast did to Beauty, she would never say such things. But her mother did not know. No one knew the real hell. Only Beauty and the Beast.

But her mother was right. She kept going back, which meant she deserved everything he did to her. Beauty felt numb as she turned onto the long gravel road to the shack in the woods. But her mind flitted with questions. How many days did she have left in her life? Would she live to see her baby grow up? Probably not. Would the Princess hate her and think she was weak like the Queen does? Or would she know that Beauty tried her best to protect her. Beauty prayed for the latter. She prayed the Princess would know how much she loved her and what she was willing to sacrifice.

22

You are never too old to set another goal or to dream a new dream...

The Beast's decline back into his own form of madness was quick and brutal. He looked at Beauty with resentment and disgust. He treated her as if every miserable moment of his life was her fault. During this time, Beauty had two more miscarriages. The Beast would work to impregnate her, then, when he found out she was pregnant, he treated her like the baby was her fault. He would accuse her of trying to trap him. He started fights, followed by beatings that would lead to the miscarriage.

Each day, Beauty fell into a darker despair. Her health declined, and she was in the emergency room over a hundred times in a six-month period, for unexplained injury or illness. The Beast was always right by her side, playing the concerned, loving husband, shooting her a "do not say a word" look and squeezing her hand hard whenever her injuries were questioned. He took her to different hospitals, so as not to raise suspicion.

During this time, Beauty had suffered multiple broken bones, and two surgeries. The Beast would sit back and watch with pleasure as others fixed the mess he made. He started to look like a gaunt version of his former self. The Beast must have lost at least thirty pounds and the face Beauty had found handsome when she met him, was now covered in "Meth sores." He was lucky to still have his perfectly white teeth, but they were beginning to have small brown stains at the bottom of the front ones. Everything was declining very quickly, and Beauty was lost in the whirlwind of chaos and pain.

The Princess spent most of her time with the Queen and King at this point. Beauty had to go visit her daughter at her Mother's house if she wanted to see her. Her typical day consisted of the Beast taking her to work, picking her up, dropping her at the Queen's to spend two hours at the most with the Princess, while he scored drugs or did whatever else vile things he was into. Then, he would pick up Beauty who cried every time she left her child. Once she got home, the Beast would rage and take out all his frustrations, misery, and anger on her. He had become more creative in abusing her, especially during sex.

Beauty felt like she was his plaything to train on. He would try something he saw on the internet and decide if it was something he wanted to do again. Each day, Beauty cried because she had once again been reduced to a monster's possession.

During those dark days, Beauty functioned like a walking Zombie, coming to life only in the presence of her daughter. She had lost almost everything, but her job and her life. Beauty did not know or understand why she stayed and endured. Something in her had become so twisted and sick she felt like a wild Beast herself.

His truck was repossessed. In a rage, he went to the lot where it was being kept and

knifed all the tires, slashed the interior, and
caused enough damage that it would cost the
dealer a great deal to resell it. This caused the
local police to charge him with Criminal Mis-
chief. A clear violation of his probation. Beauty
worried more when the Beast became more par-
anoid and secluded. He only left the house to
drive Beauty to and from work. He insisted on
watching the Princess himself to save money.
Beauty hated leaving her sweet little Princess
with the Beast. She did not trust him with her.
She asked the Queen or King to check on them
daily or take the Baby, so she would not be
alone with the Beast.

One day, while Beauty was at work, the
Queen called Beauty to tell her that the Princess
told the King that, "Daddy was watching naked
people on his phone and touching his privates
with the bathroom door open." Beauty felt sick
to her stomach and like a complete failure as a
mother. She asked the King, who had retired, to
please watch the Princess from now on. She was
not to be left with the Beast. He was worse than
Beauty thought.

Just when she thought he had gone as low
as he can go, he did something worse. His abuse
had always been directed at Beauty, and she ig-

norantly assumed that he would not hurt the Princess in any way. Deep down, she knew what he was capable of, but had held out hope it would not bleed over onto the Princess. Beauty would never understand just how deep the wickedness of the Beast ran.

The Beast got a summons to meet his probation officer about the recent charge, and he knew that he could be headed to jail. Instead of facing it like a man, he decided to run like a coward. This required Beauty and the Princess to move once again.

Everything was loaded into a moving truck in the cover of night and placed in storage. They bounced from hotel to hotel until Beauty found a small two-bedroom apartment. They only had a mattress, TV, and black curtains on every window. The Beast's paranoia was fueled by the drugs. With only one vehicle and the Beast not allowing Beauty to drive, he still drove her to and from work. That was the only time he left the apartment. He would drop Beauty off at work and then go run with his drug buddies. She was not sure what he did, exactly, when he was gone. She had her suspicions though, because one night, while he slept, she lay awake staring at the ceiling. The pain from a recent brutal rape made her insides ache. His phone was beside his head and she saw it blinking. It was a text message from a female drug dealer with a limp. Beauty only knew of this woman and her disability because the Beast had become friends with her on social media and made it a point to tell Beauty about his connection.

The text was vile.

"Sure, we can trade. The kids can play while we do it."

When Beauty scrolled up and read the conversation, she saw the Beast was offering to exchange sex with the dealer for drugs, and he was offering to do it while the Princess was with him. Beauty thought that old feeling of surprise at the extent of how far he would go would creep in and shock her, but it didn't. She felt nothing but a greater need to protect the Princess from this monster. She would find an excuse to have the Princess stay with the Queen more. Beauty was losing her child to protect her, but what choice did she have? Unless the Beast got caught or died, she was stuck with his sadistic ass. When had she become so immune to this kind of life? Her actions had become so unlike her. She really was not a person anymore.

23

Down, down, down. Would the fall never come to an end?

That day started out like any other. Beauty woke before dawn, dressed in the dark and the Beast began their drive to her job. He had been on the run from the law for about four months at this point. The Beast always drove too fast. He had no driver's license. He had lost it before Beauty met him, and he never applied for a new one. Still, he pushed the limits. It was just another way for him to follow his own rules. The Beast believed no one had the right to tell him what to do. Beauty mentioned his speeding, when it happened, but he never listened and that day, it would be his downfall.

The red and blue lights lit up the darkness behind them and the Beast tensed. It was dark in the vehicle, the only illumination coming from the red and blue lights. Beauty could see actual fear in the Beast's face. For a moment, she thought he might try to outrun the police.

"Unbuckle, we are switching places."

Beauty stared at him, dumbstruck.

"What?"

His shout echoed in the small space.

"I said unbuckle, bitch, we are switching places. They will not ask for my ID if I am not driving."

Beauty did as she was told and slid across the console and onto the Beast's lap. As she took the wheel and put her foot on the gas, the Beast slipped into the passenger seat. They managed to switch without losing speed. Beauty buckled her seatbelt and began to slow down. As she pulled over to the side of the road, the Beast appeared calm and innocent.

A tall, young officer approached Beauty's window.

"Ma'am, do you know why you are being pulled over?"

Beauty smiled politely.

"No, Sir."

The officer's face softened at Beauty's smile.

"You were going sixty-three on a fifty-five."

Beauty tried to look remorseful. "Oh, I am sorry, Officer. I am running late for work and did not realize I was speeding."

The policeman nodded with understanding. "I need your license and insurance, please."

"Sure, Officer, no problem." Beauty handed him what he needed, and he headed back to his police cruiser.

The Beast seemed to visibly relax a little.

The wait for the officer to return seemed to take forever. When he finally approached Beauty's window again, he handed her ID and insurance back without a word. She met his eyes. She could see something in them. It was then she noticed a second officer approaching the passenger side. She glanced in her side mirror and saw another police cruiser. When had that arrived? Her officer sounded very monotoned.

"I am just giving you a warning today."

Beauty smiled. "Thank you, Sir, I promise to slow it down."

Before she could start the vehicle, the officer

approaching the passenger side opened the Beast's door.

"Can you step out of the vehicle, Sir?"

The Beast shot Beauty a killing look as he unbuckled his belt and stepped out. Beauty could hear the new officer questioning the Beast.

"Do you have ID?"

"No, Sir. I was not driving, why do you need my ID?"

"What is your name?"

The Beast hesitated and gave the officer his name. He was named after his father and did not add the second. Beauty knew the Beast hoped the officer would see his father's information and assume it was him. She knew better.

"Can you walk over to the car with me while I run your information?"

The Beast followed the officer, never looking back at Beauty.

Beauty turned to the officer still standing at her window.

"I am going to open your door."

Beauty nodded mutely, unbuckled her seat belt, and turned to look at the officer. His eyes were crinkled around the edges, a pinched look on his face. Beauty had to avert her gaze. She felt like he could see all the dirty, shameful things the Beast had done to her.

Cars zoomed past as Beauty stared at her feet. Finally, the officer spoke.

"You are going to be ok now."

Beauty's brain was slow to register his words. She was going to be ok? When was the last time she was ok? Tears began to stream down her face and she stood. The officer placed a hand under her elbow to steady her. It was then she glanced toward the cruisers and saw the other officer cuffing the Beast and placing him in the back of one of the cars.

Beauty almost collapsed. Was it from relief, fear, or exhaustion? She did not know. The officer closed her door and cautiously helped her away from the vehicle and to the safety of the grass beside the road. She was still crying and only managed a stilted sentence.

"How? H--How did you know?"

The officer's tone was sympathetic.

"I saw you switch places and knew something was up. I took one look at you, then him and I knew you were in trouble. When I ran your name and saw you had no record, I knew for sure it was something with him. I saw a male name on the insurance card and ran it, and his charges and pending warrant came up. So, I called in for back-up. That's what took me so long. I was waiting for him to arrive. I must ask, did he make you trade places?"

Beauty nodded.

"Yes, Sir, I had no choice."

The officer looked at Beauty, seeming to weigh if she was telling the truth. He finally nodded and gave her a tight-lipped smile.

"Ok, then you are free to go. We will deal with him from here."

Beauty glanced at the cruisers.

"He's going to jail and will not be getting out anytime soon?"

The officer nodded again.

"Yes, Ma'am. He is going straight to booking. I doubt he will get a bond since he's a flight risk."

Beauty gave the officer a small smile and wiped the tears from her face. She moved toward her vehicle in a daze. All that kept running through her brain was the word *free*.

She was free. Beauty sat in her vehicle until both police cruisers pulled onto the road. She watched them drive away until she could no longer see their taillights. She thought, "I'm free." A broad smile spread across her face as she turned the key in the ignition.

That morning, Beauty drove herself to work for the first time in a very long time.

24

She dreamed impossible dreams, followed her heart and created her own little fairy-tale...

With a renewed sense of hope, Beauty quickly made a new life for her and the Princess. The Beast tried calling, but Beauty changed her number. She got a job seventy-miles away from where the Beast was serving his sentence, and one hundred and sixty miles from where she had lived in hell. She found a beautiful little cottage in her new town and started the Princess in a proper pre-k private school. She smiled every day and held her

Princess tightly every chance she got. They were happy.

The holidays were approaching, and Beauty was excited about them for the first time since she had met the Beast. She had decorated their little cottage with furniture she found at second-hand stores. The Beast had not paid the storage bill, so she had lost all her expensive, antique furniture and hand-me-downs, but Beauty did not dwell on the past. She looked forward, not back, and made their little cottage a home.

The Queen would drive to visit and spend time with them. There was a renewed love between Beauty and her family. She began to feel the pieces of her soul coming back. What the Beast had done to her often creeped into her mind, but she pushed it back. Beauty refused to let his darkness taint her new light.

The Drama Queen reached out to Beauty via social media, but Beauty blocked her. Then, the Wicked Bitch of the West tried to contact her. Again, Beauty blocked the attempt. The only family member of the Beast that Beauty would speak to is his Grandmother. She was from his father's side of the family, and a sweet little woman who was genuine, and understood

Beauty's trauma. She had lived in the same situation for forty years with the Beast's grandfather.

Beauty trusted the Grandmother and her motives for reaching out to Beauty. She wanted to send the Princess a present for the holidays. Beauty said she would allow this if the Grandmother promised to never give the Beast her address. The Grandmother agreed, and Beauty allowed her to send the Princess a present.

It was shortly after the new year that the first letter arrived. The Grandmother had deceived her. Beauty called the woman to ask her why she would do such a thing. She knew what the Beast had done to Beauty and the Princess. The little old woman swore to Beauty that she had not given the Beast anything.

"Then how did he get it?" she had asked. "Please tell me you did not write it down and leave it next to the phone."

The little old lady was silent.

"Oh, how could you?" Beauty was almost in tears.

"I did not think, dear. I am so sorry. The Drama Queen was here for the holidays. She must have seen it and written it down when I was not looking."

Beauty hung up on the woman and with shaky hands, opened the letter.

My Dearest Beauty,

I love and miss you so much. I am so sorry for everything I did to you and the Princess. My time in here has made me realize what a monster I was. They're making me take classes to help with my anger issues. The doctors have also regulated my medication and I am a different person now. I want to be the man you and the Princess deserve. I got my mom to send me pictures of my girls and I look at your beautiful faces every day. I promise to be a different person. I am a different person. I love you, Beauty. I truly love you and I know I took you and our daughter for granted. I am so sorry for all of it. I am sorry for the drugs. I am sober now and can barely remember all that I did, but I know it was bad and I hurt you. I am sorry. I will never be that way again.

Love,
The Beast

Beauty let the letter fall to the floor as she felt the darkness that was the Beast creep in. She prayed he would leave her and the Princess alone. She prayed he would stay in jail forever… but most of all, she prayed that she would hear no more from the Beast. She hoped that would be the only letter she would receive.

25

If you keep on believing, the dreams that you wish will come true... NOT!

Eight-eight days. That's how long Beauty got to be happy. The letters kept coming and they were all the same. The Beast made declarations of love and promises of change. Beauty did not care. She threw them all away. After a while, she stopped reading them and went on with her happy life. She should have read the letters. If she had, she might have had time to run.

It was her birthday and she was excited to

spend it with the Princess and the Queen. The Queen had started spending so much time with Beauty and the Princess that she had rented a cottage right next door. She would come to visit for three or four days at a time and Beauty could not have been happier. They had planned a laid-back night of dinner and a girl's movie, when the knock came at the door. Beauty and the Queen shared a look. Maybe it was the sweet lady next door.

The Princess took off for the door like little children do. She was bubbling with energy as she swung the door open. Beauty was only steps behind her, when she stopped dead in her tracks.

The Beast.

The Princess looked up at him, her little hand still on the door knob.

"Daddy"?

She then looked between Beauty and the Beast. A slow weary smile crept onto the Beast's face.

"Happy Birthday, my Beauty."

The Queen had gotten up from her seat and stepped toward the door. Beauty barely registered her as she passed. Her eyes were locked with the Beast's. He had not stepped into the cottage. He stood perfectly still, staring at her. Beauty felt rooted to her spot. Her feet would not move. She felt like she was stuck in a nightmare.

Then, a grating, detestable voice came from behind the Beast.

"MY LITTLE PRINCESS! YOUR AUNTIE HAS MISSED YOU SO MUCH!"

Of course. The Drama Queen. She brought him here. The oversized woman moved past the Beast and scooped up the Princess. The little girl had no clue of the evil that held her. She just laughed and hugged her aunt who had always fawned over her. The Queen looked at Beauty and searched her face. Obviously, no one knew what to do, and they were all looking to Beauty to determine how this was going to go. What did she do? Her instinct was to grab the Princess and run, but the Beast blocked the doorway.

The Beast addressed the Queen.

"So good to see you, Queen. Thank you for taking care of my girls while I was away. Did you get my letters?"

This caught Beauty's attention and she turned to her mother.

"He sent you letters?"

The Queen nodded slowly.

"He sent me and your father letters. He apologized and said he had changed. I did not want to say anything. I was afraid it would upset you."

Beauty just gaped at her mother. The woman who had told her time and again how bad the Beast was for her.

"You should have told me, Mother. Did you know he was coming here tonight?"

The Queen shook her head vehemently.

"No, no, I knew he would probably try when he got out, but I did not know he would get out so soon. I thought we would have more time. That is why I'm next door. I knew you would need me when he came. I knew that if I was here, you would have me if you needed me."

Beauty just stared at her mother like she was a stranger. She had never told her mother the extent of what the Beast had done, so the woman had no clue what the monster was capable of.

This is not happening.

That was the last thought on Beauty's mind before the room spun and she hit the floor.

Beauty could hear the hushed murmured tones

of people trying to talk quietly. It sounded like forced, polite small talk. The Queen and the Drama Queen. The Queen could not stand the Drama Queen so that explained the forced politeness. Someone was stroking her hair and her head rested on a warm leg. She smelled him before she opened her eyes. She knew who was touching her and whose lap she rested on. Beauty did not want to open her eyes. If she opened her eyes... it would all be real.

Please God, do not let it be real. Beauty opened her eyes and stared up into the ice blue ones of the Beast. His face was fuller. He had put on weight and sobriety agreed with him. The Meth had left no scarring on his face, which was lucky for him. A slow smile started on his lips.

"There she is. My beautiful girl is awake."

Beauty shot up out of his lap and tried to shake off the groggy feeling in her head. She scooted as far from the Beast as she could and looked around the room for the Princess.

"Where's the baby?"

The Beast's tone was gentle.

"She is sleeping, baby. You scared us all pretty good and your mom took her and put her to bed."

His eyes were crinkled, and she saw a gentleness in them she had never witnessed. Not even when he had been pretending to be the Boy. She was looking at the Beast, but not looking at him. It was like another person inhabited his body. Even his mannerisms were different.

His face expressed love and tenderness, and Beauty was taken by surprise. She felt the same when he would do something so heinous she could not believe it.

Beauty felt like she was living in an alternate universe. The Beast was not the Beast. The Drama Queen was in her house and talking to her mother. Everyone was acting like this was normal.

"Excuse me, I need some fresh air."

Beauty tremblingly got to her feet, the Beast standing with her as she walked toward the door. She said nothing to the Beast. She felt like her clothing was too tight and she could not breathe. Taking big gulps of air, she tried to clear her head, but no matter how much she tried she couldn't catch her breath. She was hyperventilating and bent over, placing her hands on her knees.

Beauty did not know how long she stayed outside before the Beast joined her. She was sitting in a lawn chair, head in hands, when she felt a strong arm wrap around her shoulders. Her whole body tensed. She could feel the anxiety bubbling back up inside her. The Beast started to rub slow circles on her back. Another new sensation from a monster who had tortured her for years. She did not even know she was crying until he began to soothe her.

"Shhhh, Baby, Shhhh, it's going to be ok. I promise. I am different now. I will never hurt you again."

Beauty wanted to scream. Where was her choice? No one asked her if she wanted a changed Beast. She just wanted to live a life without fear. She would never have that life with the Beast. He could be a perfect gentleman until the day she died, and she would always be waiting for him to turn back into the Beast who had tortured her.

Sitting in the dark in a second-hand lawn chair she had bought for her new Beast-free-life, the renewed light inside Beauty began to fade again. He was never going to leave her alone. Beauty did not know what hurt worse; the physical pain he had inflicted or the feeling of having her freedom snatched from her like it had never been hers at all.

Beauty lived in a prison with no bars. Her

Warden, a monster she would never escape.

26

I'm going to write myself into a fairy-tale. I desperately need a happy ending.

The Beast kept his promises. He was not a completely different person, but he was not violent or brutal. He tried to be gentle and kind. He tried to be a good husband and father. He even got a job and kept it. Beauty was miserable, but she hid her true feelings from everyone. She was always waiting for the Beast to snap and show his true face.

The Beast wanted a tattoo for his birthday, so he got one... of Beauty, pin-up style. It covered half his back and had her name at the top in big script. The Beast was so proud of the tattoo. Beauty had to smile and pretend it did not make her want to cringe every time she saw it. Hell, the tattoo was not even good. It looked nothing like Beauty and was a waste of money. But she pretended to love it and that she was honored by it.

She was not.

Beauty got so good at playing pretend it became second nature all over again. Now, instead of pretending she was not being hurt or frightened, she was pretending not to be on the verge of a constant panic attack and unhappy.

The Beast had always been a black cloud looming over Beauty, blocking out the sunshine. With his return, he became a black cloud of bad luck. Within weeks of his return, Beauty lost her job because the company suddenly closed. This left them with no money. The Beast did not make much money at his job, so they lost the cottage. The Queen allowed them to move into her cottage and helped them financially. Beauty had to get government assistance and help from charities, just to have food for them to eat. Before, events like this would have sent the Beast spiraling into a binge of drugs, rape, and violence, but instead he was being level headed and working steady. Normally, Beauty was the one trying to hold everything together, but the Beast was making efforts to contribute. That was a first, but still, Beauty couldn't find it in herself to trust him.

To add to the string of bad luck, Beauty had a routine Pap Smear and it came back with abnormal cells. She had to see an Oncologist but had no insurance. She kept this news from the Beast. Part of her feared he would view her as wounded prey and pounce. Beauty needed a job and insurance as soon as possible. She applied for several jobs and was hired by a government outfit. The pay was not great, but the insurance was good. By the time the insurance was active, Beauty had to tell the Beast about the abnormal cells they found. His reaction floored her.

He cried. Not fake crying with fake emotions. The Beast broke down and cried real tears. He just kept repeating, "I can't lose you. I can't live without you. I love you."

Beauty did not know what to say to him and awkwardly patted his shoulder.

"It will be ok. I will be ok."

When Beauty was finally able to see the Oncologist, three months had passed. The Beast went with her to the appointment and held her hand during the biopsy. The doctor decided to remove three small sections of her cervix and did the procedure right there in the office. It was painful, but Beauty told herself she had been through way worse.

They waited two weeks for the results. Everything came back benign and a tension Beauty had not realized she had, left her. She had not allowed herself to worry about the cancer. She could not. It amazed Beauty how easily she could accept the possibility of the Beast taking her life... but to Cancer? No, she could not bring herself to consider that.

Beauty had been working for the government for about six months when she got an opportunity for promotion and a transfer closer to her family. The Beast seemed excited and supportive of the move.

Life between them had changed, and yet stayed the same in so many ways. The violence was gone. The rape was gone. But the Beast still had problems. He was an addict. Sex addict, drama addict, attention addict, drug addict, Beauty addict. His obsession with her had become stifling. The Beast wanted to talk to her, text her, be with her twenty-four seven. It was like he had given up the violence to become even more needy.

The time the Beast had spent in jail did change him. He did not have any fight in him anymore, but he still had that need to possess Beauty. He struggled with smoking pot and would find people to get it from. It was a financial strain, and Beauty worried that if he was around any kind of drug, he would go back to the hard stuff. That was the problem with an extreme addict like him. They always took the addictions to the extreme. He was a walking addiction and instability. Beauty hoped if she was closer to home, the King would help the Beast get a better job and they would be more financially stable.

Beauty only had three days to find a place to live and start her new job two hundred miles away. They loaded up a moving truck and Beauty said goodbye to the cottages. The Beast was driving the moving truck and Beauty drove her Jeep. The Beast stayed right behind Beauty the entire trip. It was the middle of the night and they were looking at a four-hour drive. The Princess lay sleeping in her car seat in the back with her mother.

Beauty was headed to her parents' home

and the closer she got, the more the memories flooded her. Her parents' home used to be Beauty's home. It was her house of horrors. The King and Queen had bought the home Beauty and the Beast had lived in when the Princess was born Her parents had no idea of the violence and rape that had taken place there. They had no idea of the pain their daughter had suffered in every room of their house. Her parents slept in the room where Beauty had been raped so violently that her blood soaked through the sheets and stained the mattress. The sink where her father brushed his teeth and washed his hands, the Beast had broken two of Beauty's ribs when he picked her up by the throat and slammed her against the faucet. Their kitchen floor was the one Beauty had fallen onto and cried on as her heart broke. There was not a single space in their home where Beauty could not recall an act of violence or emotional pain... and her parents had no idea. That had been Beauty's life, and now they were headed back to the scene of the crimes.

She wondered if returning to the house of horrors would spark something in the Beast. Would he crave that violence again? Did he crave it now and she just did not see it? Beauty did not know. The Beast was still as much a mystery now as he had been the night he had showed her his true face.

27

There's no place like home...

I t was early in the morning when they arrived at Beauty's parents' house. Dawn had not yet broken, and all of the large oak trees were casting eerie shadows across the house which held so many bad memories for Beauty. She wondered if the Beast would see it as she did, like a beacon of agony on a dead-end street. Or would he see it as his house of treasures? The place where he had enjoyed committing so many depraved acts against Beauty. Would the Beast feel remorse or longing for those days?

Beauty felt a bone deep weariness seep into

her bones as she got out of her Jeep. She had endeavored for the past few years to spend as little time as possible in the house. Now, she would be spending the night. Several nights, in fact, until they could find a home. With a heavy heart, she got the still sleeping Princess out of her seat and headed inside. She looked back at the Beast and saw a huge grin on his face. Nope, she thought. This place does not hold the same meaning for him as it did for her. He was rubbing his hands together and looked gleeful. Her voice held a tinge of suspicion.

"What are you so happy about"?

The Beast did not even try to wipe the smile from his face.

"Nothing. I'm just glad we're here. I'm excited."

She thought about asking him what he had to be excited about but decided she did not want to know. She never knew what was going on in his brain and was not sure she ever wanted to.

Beauty imagined that if someone cut open the Beast's skull and peered inside, it would be a spiraling pool of darkness tinged with blood, hate, and all the misery the world had to offer. She shook her head to clear the image. She must be delirious from lack of sleep.

With a soft knock and a smile from her mother, Beauty stepped inside the house of horrors. The Beast was right behind her, animatedly chattering away to the Queen. Beauty just wanted to lay the baby down and get some sleep herself. Maybe if she shut her eyes to her surroundings, she would forget where she was.

As she laid down beside the Beast that night and he wrapped an arm around her body, she felt an overwhelming sense of déjà vu. The Beast's whisper was a low rumble in her ear.

"We're home, Baby."

Her body tensed, and he clutched her closer.

"It's ok. Relax."

Beauty lay like that until she could no longer hold her eyelids open. The Beast's slow and steady breaths a rhythm in her ears. If she had not been so exhausted, sleep would have eluded her, but it didn't. She drifted off into a nightmare fueled darkness. All the shame of her past haunting her dreams and tormenting her.

The next morning, Beauty woke up from a nightmare, crying. A groggy Beast tried to soothe her.

"It's ok. It's ok. Shhhh, calm down. It's just

a nightmare."

It had felt so real to Beauty. It was the first time Beauty had a nightmare that felt so real. She had been trapped in a violent rape and the Beast's presence. His touch only made it worse and she recoiled from his attempts to soothe her. The house and the monster were too much for Beauty to handle.

She slipped from the bed and the Beast's grasp as quickly as she could. Beauty could not stay in this house. She left a baffled looking Beast in the bed and headed to take a shower. Even the guest bathroom held bad memories for her.

She showered and dressed as fast as she could. Beauty was on a mission. Even though it was the weekend, she needed to find another place to live.

At breakfast, everyone was laughing and talking. The Beast looked right at home in the dining room where he had once beaten Beauty so badly she had not been able to stand without serious back pain for at least a week. As Beauty sat down at the table and looked for some place to focus on that did not carry a bad memory, something the Queen was saying caught her attention.

"The house right behind ours is vacant. It has been vacant for a while now. Something weird happened with the people. The wife ran off and they abandoned the kids. The state came in and took them all... it was very sad. But it's vacant and I think it's for sale. It needs a lot of work, but wouldn't that be wonderful if y'all lived right behind us? We could have family dinners and spend time together."

Beauty vaguely recalled the house. It was a large two-story structure with a big yard. That was about the extent of what she knew about it. Not even bothering to touch the food on her plate, Beauty shot up out of her seat like her ass was on fire.

"I'll go look at it right now and see if it has a sign in the yard."

Beauty did not even wait for anyone to respond. She headed out the front door and around the side of the house. Both houses had a side facing a large open field. The cooling fall morning made Beauty wish she had brought a jacket as she walked through the field toward the house. The outside looked ok. It was older and needed some work, but anything was better than staying in the house of horrors. As Beauty approached the looming structure, she got a bad feeling but chalked that up to the proximity of the horror house. She did not see a sign in the yard, but the house looked vacant. It almost looked abandoned.

There was a detached garage and Beauty peered through one of the dusty windows. She saw a "for sale" sign leaning up against the wall of the garage. If she squinted, she could make out the phone number. It was an out of state number, but she dialed it. Beauty did not expect anyone to answer on a weekend and was surprised when a nice man did. She explained her situation, and the gentleman seemed pleasant enough and told Beauty where the key was located. He said she could look inside before she made any decisions. He explained that he lived out of state and the home had been an investment. He had never actually seen the inside of the house, but his friend, who had found it for him, said it needed a lot of work.

Beauty thanked the man and found the key. She made quick work unlocking the side door to the house. The man had not been kidding. Inside, it was a disaster. The wood flooring was half missing in the living room and there were holes in the walls. The carpet was very outdated, and the place was musky. But all in all, it had good bone structure.

The kitchen was updated, and the staircase curved, which Beauty liked. There was a big back porch and a large yard for the Princess to play in. Even though Beauty liked the house, she could not shake the bad vibes she felt from it. She was just locking up when the Beast appeared.

"I see you found a key."

"Yes, and I spoke with the owner. He wanted me to look inside and call him back."

The Beast motioned for Beauty to unlock the door.

"Let me have a look."

Beauty quietly stood back as the Beast went through every room in the home. He checked out the yard, garage, and even discovered a small apartment off the garage, that Beauty had not noticed. When he was done, and Beauty was locking the door, she turned to him expectantly.

"Well?"

A huge grin spread across the Beast's face.

"I love it! Call the man back and tell him we will take it!"

Beauty eyed the Beast.

"You did not get any bad feelings from it?"

The Beast chuckled and wrapped an arm around Beauty's waist as he scoffed.

"No, Baby. Damn, you are so superstitious. I love it. Let's take it!"

Against her better judgement, Beauty did as she was told and called the man back. He emailed her the paperwork and said they could move in right away. So that is what they did.

Beauty and the Beast spent that evening moving into their new home. That night, the Princess stayed with the Queen, and Beauty tired herself out unpacking boxes by candle-light. She had one day before she started her new job.

In the eerie old house surrounded by boxes, Beauty watched the shadows of the candlelight dance against the wall. That feeling of dread had never left. Something bad had happened in this house. Beauty could feel it. She was so en-thralled in her thoughts she did not hear the Beast, until he wrapped his arms around her from behind and whispered in her ear.

"We're all alone. Let's christen our new home." Beauty's insides clinched with fear and she cringed.

"Sure, Honey, let me just finish this box up and I will see you in bed."

The Beast flung the box away and smiled down at her in such a way that the hairs on the back of her neck stood up.

"Finish it tomorrow. I want my Beauty now."

28

Make a fairy-tale and go live in it...

Beauty was nervous on her first day at her new job. Everyone seemed nice but whenever her boss was not around, the others gave her pitying glances. Beauty did not understand why everyone acted like working for Maleficent was such a hardship. She liked the woman's hard-nosed approach. Hew new boss was efficient and expected the same of her employees. Beauty could respect that. It was work, not a place to be paid to socialize.

Beauty was to be Maleficent's assistant and help her keep the unit running as smoothly as possible. Her office was directly across the hall, so the woman could holler if she wanted anything. Other people scoffed at this, but Beauty had worked with and for far more demanding people.

She shared the office with two women she instantly liked. Both were beautiful and fierce in their own ways. Nala was statuesque and quiet, with a beautiful smile. She was the grapevine for all the happenings in the office, because everyone knew she was trustworthy and kind hearted. Tiana was tiny like Beauty but fierce like a mama lion. She had the best laugh and took no shit from anyone. Tiana made Beauty laugh every day and both women reminded Beauty what it had been like to have friends. It had been so long since Beauty had any friends. She could never have them as friends outside of work, because she was not allowed friends, but these women made Beauty look forward to each day.

They did not know it, but their kindness and laughter made Beauty's life a little easier. When she was around them, the constant anxiety over the Beast and her other troubles would melt away.

Beauty was happy at work. She could be a

little more of herself. She liked everything and everyone in the office. Well, not everyone. She did not like the strange, orange-haired witch who had transferred right before Beauty. She was older than Beauty and there was something a little off about her. She immediately sensed the same manic personality as the Beast, and the same fake charm as well.

The red-haired witch was a phony, except in her one strange obsession. The witch was obsessed with someone name Mr. Knight. He was a sailor deployed overseas. Beauty was responsible for making sure his time was put into the schedule, but she had never met the man. He was all the red-haired witch talked about. It was the way the witch talked about him that creeped Beauty out. A glimmer in the woman's eyes and the way she spoke of the man, as if he was a God, was very familiar to Beauty.

Beauty set the conversations aside and avoided the strange woman whenever possible, but every time she saw Mr. Knight's name on something, she would think to herself, "Hmmm, Mr. Knight, what is so freaking fantastic about you that this crazy woman is obsessed?"

Beauty knew she was in a predominately female line of work and men were scarce, but the witch's fascination was more than just infatuation. It was like Mr. Knight was the only reason the witch had to live. Every time he would respond to one of her emails, the witch would be giddy with joy, running around the office and telling anyone who would listen, "I heard from Mr. Knight, yada yada yada." This was usually when Beauty tuned her out. People were polite about it, but finally one day, Beauty asked Nala and Tiana.

"What's her deal? Isn't she married?"

Tiana laughed her glorious laugh. Nala just raised an eyebrow and stayed reservedly quiet.

"Girl, she's crazy about that man. Rumor has it they're a thing, but I don't think they are. I think she wishes they were and likes to lead people to believe they have a relationship. But it always seemed one-sided to me. Besides, have you seen her? Mr. Knight is much younger than her and she has a husband. A boat load of kids and problems. But, you didn't hear that from me."

Beauty giggled, then thought about what Tiana had said.

"How much younger?"

"I don't know, probably closer to your age."

Beauty nodded and that was the extent of her conversation with the girls about the mysterious Mr. Knight.

For the next year, Beauty would see his name and hear the witch's stories about him. Every time, Beauty and Tiana would share a look and a grin after the red-haired witch left to flit around the office and blather on about the incredible Mr. Knight. Beauty felt like she knew him even though they had never met. It was a strange feeling to Beauty, like hearing stories of a distant relative you had never seen a picture of and would never meet.

During this year the Beast withdrew from Beauty. The King had gotten the Beast a very good job and they should have been financially stable... but they were not. The Beast's drug habit affected their ability to make ends meet. As far as Beauty knew, he was not back into the hard stuff again, but he was obsessed with and only concerned about smoking pot. It was his obsession of choice now. Not Beauty or the Princess. It was like he checked out. There was no violence or rape. There was just... nothing.

At some point, the Beast went off his medication and started self-medicating with the pot.

She figured he stayed perpetually stoned to feel nothing. If he could not feel his depraved impulses, then he wanted to feel nothing at all. The only time he showed a hint of the real Beast was when he was running low on pot, but thankfully, he always found a way to be "medicated."

The Beast made a set of friends at work who was into smoking pot and getting stoned as well, so if he was out, one of them always had something. This led to the Beast spending very little time at home. He worked a three to eleven shift, but he would leave around ten a.m. and not come home until after two or three in the morning. Beauty was glad for it at first. This meant she did not have to pretend as often. She only saw the Beast asleep or on the weekends.

Beauty hated the weekends because the Beast was always in a foul mood and could not wait to get back to work. She knew it was his friends he wanted to get back to. He did a horrible job of hiding his misery. Every weekend it was the same thing. He would sleep until late in the day, wake up, get high, then complain about being bored at home. Eventually, he would eat up all the food in the house before getting high again. Complain some more and go to sleep.

The Beast had become the most miserable

son of a bitch Beauty had ever known. It was a new kind of emotional abuse and stress on Beauty. She had been reduced to nothing in a unique way. She might as well have been a ghost or inanimate object as far as the Beast was concerned.

When he had returned, a less violent man, he had been obsessed with Beauty. She had grown used to the attention and thought in a twisted way that he loved her. Now, his attention had been removed and she was ignored. Another mind-fuck from the king of them. She did not know if it was deliberate, to hurt her, or just his own personal misery with life. After six years, Beauty still did not understand the Beast. She didn't believe she ever would. How can anyone understand the insanity of a madman's mind? It would be years later before the Beast would tell Beauty exactly how he felt.

His exact words to Beauty were arrogant and completely Beast worthy.

"I never loved you, Beauty. I thought you were annoying and got on my fucking nerves. I could not stand you, to the point where any time you got in the car and started to run your mouth, I wanted to shoot myself. You were just some Bitch I knocked up and felt stuck with. I resented you for being pregnant and felt like you stole my twenties from me. I wish I had taken the out you offered and never looked back."

The Beast loved very few things. Beautiful, curvy women, drugs, and fast cars. It did not have to be in that order. Since he was making more money and even though they could not afford it with his drug habit, the Beast got a sports car and suddenly, he wasn't so miserable. The addition of his new "Baby" meant Beauty was now completely replaced, and the Beast had an excuse to be gone on the weekends. He got into illegal street racing. This fact both delighted and terrified Beauty. The Beast had no license, but no one could tell him anything. He never learned anything from his mistakes, but Beauty could not make him do anything or learn anything. She was delighted because he seemed less miserable which made her life less miserable. Beauty was terrified because it was dangerous, and she was afraid the Beast would hurt someone.

He had changed by removing the violence, but he was still an addict with obsessive tendencies. Beauty did not know if this was because he was bipolar and manic-depressive or just so damaged he knew no other way.

Once the car was in the picture, Beauty rarely saw the Beast. His life revolved around drugs and his beloved car. She went from one kind of loveless marriage to another and both were far from what she had imagined for herself. Beauty and the Princess were just an afterthought to the Beast. If he even thought of them at all anymore.

29

And just like that, her heart began to beat...

It was a warm, late summer morning. Beauty was standing outside her office talking with the girls when she looked up and stilled. Everything around her stilled. Time moved at a snail's pace like someone had pushed a slow-motion button on her life. A tall, very well-built and handsome, dark-haired man approached. He was wearing a navy-blue polo shirt and khaki pants. The shirt was stretched against his muscled chest and biceps.

Her gaze swept over him from feet to head. She could see a tattoo peeking out beneath the sleeve of one arm. The man was adjusting his shirt and looking downward so Beauty could not tell anything about his face. As he walked straight in her direction, his head lifted, and their eyes met. Beauty's breath caught in her throat. He was dashingly handsome, with a strong jaw, straight nose and the most beautiful eyes; a kaleidoscope of dark blues, light blues, and gray. Beauty had never seen eyes like his. She must have looked dumbstruck but quickly recovered, as a slow lazy smile spread across his beautiful mouth. It was a perfect mouth with the bottom lip just a tiny bit fuller and the top lip curved with a little divot above the bow. The man had an easiness about him that made Beauty feel instantly safe in his presence. She had never felt anything like what she was feeling. It was like an instant connection. She felt like she had known this stranger her whole life and knew that he would never hurt her. After an awkward silence, the stranger gave a little wave and nod toward Beauty, that stunning smile on his face.

"Hi, I'm Mr. Knight. Nice to meet you."

Beauty's first thought was, "Oh my Gods. I finally get the witch's strange obsession."

Mr. Knight looked at her expectedly. Was

she gawking? Had she been silent too long? Oh, right, he introduced himself. Beauty extended her hand.

"I'm Beauty, nice to meet you too."

When he wrapped his large hand around Beauty's small one, tingles spread up her arm, down her body, and straight into her toes. His voice was pleasant and soothing.

"You must be new. Before I was deployed, I worked at another office, but it has since shut down. They're transferring me to a smaller office, but I will be here until it's ready."

All Beauty could do was smile and nod at Mr. Knight. She was completely mesmerized by him and felt a bit foolish for acting like a giddy school girl.

Beauty, Mr. Knight, and the girls, all headed inside the office. He held the door open for them like the true southern gentleman he was. Beauty glanced over her shoulder once and felt her cheeks flush as he gave her a shy smile. She smiled back and quickly headed to her office.

Mr. Knight had to meet with the boss Maleficent, so Beauty started her day. She was barely into her daily routine when the boss called her out into the hallway and instructed her to help Mr. Knight get set up on one of the available computers, and to make sure he gets anything he needs. Beauty was right on that task with pep in her step.

As she escorted Mr. Knight to a training room with extra computers, they made basic small talk. She asked about his service and thanked him for it. He was humble and kind, with such a sweet easy-going personality. He was the exact opposite of the Beast.

As Beauty got Mr. Knight settled in, she felt a pang at having to leave his presence, and a little embarrassed that she might have seemed like a simpering fool.

As she left the room, she turned to look back at his handsome visage one last time and found him smiling up at her from his seat. His muscled frame looked too large for the desk chair, but it was his eyes that made her pause. He was smiling that mega-watt smile, and tiny crinkles had formed around the corners of those magnificent blue eyes. They were the kindest eyes Beauty had ever seen. Something strange had happened in her heart. A flutter, like it had skipped a beat, and she felt a lump lodge in her throat. She managed a small smile before she had to duck her head and slip out with a wave.

That day, Beauty must have walked by that

conference room ten times just to sneak a peek at Mr. Knight. For the first time in a long time, maybe for the first time ever, Beauty felt like she was walking on clouds... and that day, she was happy. All because of Mr. Knight's smile.

That was how the next week of Beauty's life went. Mr. Knight was in the office every day and she was a little lighter and happier because of his presence. They rarely spoke. It was just a few shared smiles and waves here and there. Beauty wanted to gag and vomit whenever she heard the red witch's boisterous laughter or loud mouth coming down the hallway. The witch seemed to be on her own manic version of cloud nine with Mr. Knight around. Her dislike and distrust of that witch grew in droves in those few short days.

Unfortunately, Beauty's happiness would be short-lived. Mr. Knight was sent hours away for training, for the next two and half to three months. Beauty felt a sense of loss over a man she barely knew. A kind of ache to be near him again... but she shook it off. She was married to a vile Beast and surely Mr. Knight did not feel the same connection Beauty did. She was probably just a lonely, abused woman in need of affection, and he was an attractive man. At least, that's what Beauty told herself every time she thought of Mr. Knight or sent him an extra smiley face through work correspondence.

Summer had ended, the Beast was the same, Mr. Knight was far away, and life went back to normal for Beauty. However, as fall was underway, and the autumn leaves had started to turn, Beauty was offered a job opportunity and promotion. She would be promoted and paid more but must move to a new office. All of this was fine with Beauty, because that meant a shorter drive and more time with the Princess, although she would miss her book boyfriends. She had become very fond of listening to her audiobooks on the hour to and from work each day. She listened at work as well. People would always comment about how Beauty constantly had earphones on.

Beauty had always loved books, but the Beast had ruined her eyesight with head trauma. So, she began listening to audiobooks rather than read. She very quickly found herself immersed in the lives of the wonderful heroes and heroines of the books. Somewhere along the way, the books became Beauty's escape from reality. If she was listening to a book, she could block out all the bad thoughts and get lost in a character's wonderful life.

It was nearing the holidays and Beauty's last day with the unit had arrived. It fell on the staff meeting day, so they threw Beauty a going-away party. She was going to miss all her friends, but was looking forward to the new challenges ahead, and the better pay. She had just taken her seat at the table and went to take a bite from her sparsely filled plate, when she felt a familiar presence sit down beside her. Out of the corner of her eye, she saw that it was Mr. Knight. He was back, and still looked as good as he had that week she got to spend around him.

Beauty suddenly lost her appetite, too embarrassed to eat, which was not something that had ever happened before. Mr. Knight leaned close to her and she breathed in his clean scent. *Damn, he smells good*, her foggy brain barely registered. His voice was low, barely above a whisper. He was obviously using a polite and respectable level for the professional meeting.

"You are going to like the smaller office. I really like it."

Beauty nodded and barely managed a glance and polite smile in his direction. Her brain had just gone into meltdown mode.

Then it sunk in. "Oh crap! Holy Shit!"

Mr. Knight would be in the new office.

Had she not realized that, or was that fact one of her considerations when she accepted the job? Beauty did not know the answer. Maybe she was too scared to admit that she wanted to be closer to him. Either way, as she sat there next to Mr. Knight, occasionally stealing a glance his way and being rewarded with one of his heart stopping smiles, Beauty felt something new grow inside her heart. With Mr. Knight's proximity, Beauty was feeling a mix of excitement, fear, and that strange feeling she could not put her finger on.

One thought repeated in her head. "This is going to be a big problem."

30

Down, down, down the Rabbit Hole. Princesses, passion, and more issues than Vogue...

O h yes, it was indeed going to be a BIG problem!

That was Beauty's first thoughts as she stepped into her new office for the first time. She was greeted with kindness by two uniquely beautiful women, one older, guarded woman, and Mr. Knight.

Jasmine had that petite, curvy build most women coveted. Her dark hair fell in waves midway down her back, with layers that sat perfectly on her small shoulders. She had big, dark eyes with lush lashes and a flawless olive completion. Beauty sensed a nonsense toughness underlying the infectious smile on the woman's face. She liked her immediately and could tell they would be fast friends. Jasmine was beautiful, strong, genuine, and funny. All qualities Beauty admired.

Aurora had stunning golden streaks mixed into her light brown hair. She was friendly with a polite smile and a down-to-earth personality that put Beauty at ease. She too seemed sincere and real. Beauty felt she could find friendship with both women. Hopefully like what she had shared with Nala and Tiana.

With a measuring look and efficient tone, the guarded woman introduced herself.

"I'm Mama Odie. I have been here the longest, and your office is right next to mine."

Mama Odie did not extend her hand but did give Beauty a slightly terrifying smile. *This one is going to be watching me like a hawk and reporting everything to the boss.* Mama Odie gestured for Beauty to follow her. She offered the woman a polite nod and with a quick wave to the others, headed down a hallway to her new office.

The building was older, with yellowed linoleum floors, drab walls, and wood paneling. Beauty did not care because she had her own office. When Mama Odie gestured toward Beauty's office door and she stepped into her own office, Beauty offered a quick "thank you" and a polite wave.

Her office was quaint, with a sliver of a window and only the bare necessities. Beauty smiled at her new L-shaped wooden desk and standard office chair. The walls had no personality yet, but Beauty loved it.

"I can work with this," she thought and set her belongings on the shorter side of the desk. She had two computer screens, two old chairs that were still in fair condition, fronting her desk for client interviews, and a phone. Everything she needed to get the job done. Except maybe, simple office supplies. She would have to find the supply closet soon.

Beauty had just taken a seat when a slight knock came at the door. There was a long, thin window on the door that she could see through, and Beauty could see a tall figure on the other side. Her heart began to do that fluttering thing.

"Come in."

The door opened slowly, and Mr. Knight's handsome frame filled the doorway. That heart stopping smile on his gorgeous face.

Beauty's brain did a stutter step. *SHIT, SHIT, SHIT, Get it together, idiot*. She pasted a smile on her face.

"Hi." That was all she could mutter.

His mega-watt smile only faltered enough to greet her back and then returned full force. They were looking at each other like a pair of grinning idiots. Her, more so than him, she was sure. Beauty cleared her throat.

"What's up?"

He stepped into her office and seated his muscled frame into one of the client chairs. Beauty was trying to wipe the smile off her face and come across as professional but was probably only succeeding in looking like she had a facial tick or was on the verge of a stroke. Mr. Knight looked at ease. He was the kind of guy who looked at ease no matter what he was doing.

Beauty wondered how at ease he would look naked. She could feel her face flushing with heat. She was probably turning a cherry red. "Oh my God, where had that thought come from?" She had not thought of anyone naked in years. She was so used to seeing the Beast and only the Beast that she was numb to sexual arousal. Her cheeks heated further, and she could feel a flush spreading down her neck. *FUCK, FUCK, DOUBLE FUCK!* Mr. Knight was looking at her, his eyebrow quirked.

What the fuck was wrong with her? This man is going to think she has mental deficiencies if she keeps staring, grinning and turning beet red. Beauty tried to school her face and cleared her throat. With a cock of her head, she indicated that Mr. Knight start. His voice sounded like he was holding in a chuckle and trying to sound professional.

"I just stopped by to let you know the boss called and assigned me to be your trainer. Looks like you will be shadowing me all day, every day, until it's time for your own out of town training." The mega-watt smile returned, and Beauty's eyes just about bugged out of her head.

TRIPLE FUCK, SHIT, I AM DOOMED. Her mouth was wise enough not to blurt out what she was thinking. Instead, she said, "I need pencils." She was mortified and got diarrhea of the mouth whenever she was nervous. "I also need pens, paper, notebooks, and highlighters."

Mr. Knight nodded slowly, his eyebrows drawn together, a slight frown on his lips, as if he was processing her strange behavior.

"Ok." The word was drawn out as his gorgeous kaleidoscope eyes met Beauty's hazel ones. She just about melted, and she knew an unconscious dreamy grin had spread across her face.

With his own answering grin, Mr. Knight said, "Follow me. The supply closet is right across from my office."

Beauty jumped up from her chair like something had bitten her. "Crap," she thought. "This man makes me act like a lovestruck school girl. Get it together, Beauty."

As she followed Mr. Knight to his office on the other side of the building, he made steady small talk about the job. Beauty heard none of it. She was too busy trying to focus on not falling on her face and overcoming the weak-kneed effect he had on her.

Beauty was baffled. Never in her life had any man ever had this kind of effect on her. Not once, even when she was younger and a famous young actor tried to pick her up in a casino. That guy had been gorgeous and from a famous family, but Beauty had declined gracefully and even spent two hours talking with the guy before sending him off to his room, ALONE. Beauty had treated him like a normal person and never once felt awe-struck by him and she had seen all his movies. What was the deal with Mr. Knight?

Beauty was so lost in her thoughts that she ran right into him. He was like a brick wall of muscle and she lost her balance. He quickly whirled around to steady her before she fell right onto her butt. His hands were large and warm on Beauty's arms. She could feel the warmth through the long cotton sleeves of her undershirt. Beauty wanted to sigh and lean into him. He felt so comfortable and safe, and he smelled so good... like soap coffee and real man. An actual man, not a monster.

"You ok?" His concerned eyes skimmed her from head to toe.

Beauty had to will herself to step out of his embrace.

"Yes, yes, I am fine. Sorry about my clumsiness. I should watch where I am going."

That slow, sly grin that she was already beginning to love the sight of crept across his face. He was so real. Nothing fake about him like the asshole, Beast. Mr. Knight had the best smiles, the kind that made his eyes twinkle. Really twinkled like nothing she had ever seen before. There was just something about him, as if he possessed all things good in the world. Everything about him was light and goodness. The complete opposite and a stark contrast to the Beast's darkness and tainted love.

Beauty shook the thoughts from her head and tried to focus on supplies. She side-stepped Mr. Knight and gathered up all the supplies she thought she might need, even grabbing some extra so she wouldn't have to make another trip to the closet. Beauty feared she might do something embarrassing like fall on her face if she had to walk past Mr. Knight to get supplies.

Once done, Beauty tried to slip out of the closet and back to her office, but Mr. Knight, being the gentleman he was, waited and helped her carry her supplies. She walked with her head held high and arms full. Praying she won't trip and make a fool of herself. Mr. Knight was close on her heels.

She dumped her supplies on her desk and set out to organizing everything. Mr. Knight did the same and Beauty looked at him with questions in her eyes. He quirked his brows again as if to say, "What, I can't help?" Then came the grinning fool routine. This man had to think she was some kind of village idiot.

As she finished with the last of her supplies, Mr. Knight grabbed a note pad and pen.

"Are you ready? I think this is all you will need for notes."

Beauty was giddy, an effect his nearness had on her. She nodded a reply and followed him back to his office. It looked the same as Beauty's, but bigger. The desk was smaller, and he had no windows, but everything else seemed the same as Beauty's office. Mr. Knight sat down in his office chair and Beauty took a seat across from him in one of the client chairs. She was glad to have some distance. Her back was ramrod straight and starting to ache from trying to hold a proper posture. The silence dragged on as he typed away at his keyboard and talked to Beauty about how to use the computer systems. She was not hearing a word he said. All Beauty heard was the pounding of her heart as she watched his muscles flex with each movement of his body.

"Good God," she thought. "Is his office getting hotter or is that just me?" She tried to discreetly fan her face.

Mr. Knight was in the middle of talking about something and must have noticed the glazed look in her eyes. He stopped and stared at her. Then, he leaned back in his chair and laced the fingers of his large hands behind his head. He was eyeing Beauty and she felt like a bug under a microscope. Before she could say anything to break the tension, Mr. Knight shot up out of his chair as if struck by a stroke of genius. Beauty just watched in silence as he dragged the other client chair and placed it right beside his, behind the desk. With a grin, he motioned for her to take a seat. RIGHT NEXT TO HIM. Like arms touching next to him.

Beauty looked from him to the chair then back again several times, before finally standing. She trembled as she approached the chair. Mr. Knight gave her one of his heart-stopping smiles and looked at her as if he had just solved the world's hardest puzzle.

Like a gentleman, he waited for her to be seated and then took his own. She was sitting a little behind and to the side of him, so he had to look over one broad shoulder or turn in his seat to face her, whenever he wanted to point out something he thought was particularly important or helpful. Which was ridiculous... because Beauty heard none of it.

Between the smell of him and her straying thoughts, she did well in keeping her face looking professional. But it was a struggle. She nodded when he glanced at her and pretended she was following. He would nod back and reward her with one of his dazzling smiles which would make her insides tingle. The whole time he spoke, Beauty was just enjoying the southern cadence of his voice. She was also admiring every inch of him, hoping she did not get caught.

Before she knew it, it was the end of the day, and Beauty felt a pang of sadness in her chest at the thought of being far of his presence. As she got up to leave, he surprised her with out-stretched arms.

"Good job today. How about a hug?"

Beauty went into his arms without pause and breathed in his scent like her life depended on it. His arms were large and engulfed her in a way that made her feel protected. The hug was brief, but instantly, Beauty knew she would for-ever crave and miss that feeling. She had to force herself to walk away from him.

As Beauty drove home that evening, she was in a fog. In her mind, she analyzed every word and gesture he made while they worked together. Trying to determine if he was just be-ing friendly or if he also felt something. He was so reserved and easy-going that Beauty could not get a read on any of his actions.

By the time she pulled into her driveway, she still had no answers. Frustrated and tired, she was glad the Beast was not home. That night, as she put the beautiful Princess to sleep, Beauty decided she would figure Mr. Knight out and deal with whatever the outcome would be. If he felt the same, she would not deny him. If he did not, she would suffer in silence like she had been doing for years.

The next morning, Beauty was in a good mood. She took extra care with her appearance and set off to work with a spring in her step. She decided to test Mr. Knight and gauge his reactions. Beauty never had to seduce a man or even pursue one.

Over the next few weeks, she put an extra sway in her hips, and wore professional but feminine attire that accentuated her figure without being provocative. Beauty found reasons to touch him or be near him during their training. A brush of the hand or touch of the thigh as she scooted closer. He never tensed at her touch or scooted away at her nearness. Beauty also opened herself up to friendly banter. Maybe it was flirting, she was not sure. It was her brand of flirting. Beauty and Mr. Knight would get sidetracked talking about personal likes and dislikes. She found they had a lot in common, and the more she learned about the man, the more she liked him. She still got giddy in his presence, but with time, the nervousness turned into an ease she had never known with any man. He was a handsome, strong, kind, and humble person. Everything the Beast was not. She never talked to Mr. Knight about the Beast, but she often shared stories about the Princess, and he seemed genuinely interested in her daughter. It delighted Beauty whenever he would ask about the Princess or when she shared photos and could see his true delight over them.

Beauty could feel the bond growing with each passing day. She also felt hope growing inside her too. If she could find love with someone like Mr. Knight, maybe she was not lost to the Beast after all. With Mr. Knight by her side, she could escape the Beast once and for all.

The days were spent laughing, learning and exchanging enjoyable conversation as they grew closer. At the end of each day, they hugged, and that hug carried Beauty until the next day when she could be near him again. They had exchanged phone numbers and texted outside of work, but it was all innocent and polite small talk. They were friends and he was being a helpful one. That's what Beauty told herself.

She could not let herself get lost in the fantasy of more... when her reality was so bleak. She could not handle any more heartbreak.

Mr. Knight never spoke of a relationship, but he wore a ring. This bothered Beauty, until finally, one day, she asked him if he had a wife.

"Yes, I do."

Beauty's heart sank, and she tried to mask the stab of pain she felt in her chest.

"Oh, how did you meet?"

Mr. Knight sounded so matter of fact when he told her. He seemed very detached from the whole subject.

"When I was young, I had two friends I hung out with. She was their cousin who was always around. I never really paid much attention to her. I was not interested in a relationship and it just kind of happened. When I left to go off to school, she followed. She kind of never went away. When I joined the service, and was involuntarily mobilized, I thought it was best we marry so she would be taken care of in case something happened to me."

Beauty blinked. "Well, isn't that just the most romantic thing she had ever heard. NOT!" she thought.

"Umm... Ok. Do you have a photo of her?"

Mr. Knight pulled out his phone, tapped and swiped a few times, then turned the screen to face her. Beauty barely kept the cringe off her face. The woman looked like an Ogre. Beauty was not judgmental, but she had expected a tiny, blonde bombshell she could never compete with. She had not expected a bitchy looking troll.

Mr. Knight turned the phone back around and tucked it away on the desk. Beauty could not read the emotions on his face, but she sensed unhappiness and detachment on his part. Her mind raced. "Could he be unhappy in a loveless marriage like she was?"

Beauty did not want to get her hopes up or break up a marriage, but she found herself prying about the Troll.

"Everything ok? With the wife, I mean."

Mr. Knight was silent as he stared at the computer. His finger on his right hand clicked through the screens. She thought maybe she had overstepped, then he began to speak.

"She is very spoiled and lazy. She doesn't

work. I work all day, come home and have to mow with the tractor. Clean the house, then cook and make dinner. She doesn't do anything but sleep late, get up, eat, and watch TV until two in the morning."

Beauty was taken aback at his honest admission and the utter laziness of the troll. She had always been hard-working and independent. She didn't understand someone who could be so lazy. Before she could stop herself, she blurted out with bewilderment.

"She does not do anything? You have to do EVERYTHING?" Her voice rose a little with the last word.

Mr. Knight turned to look at her, sadness in those kaleidoscope eyes.

"Yes."

"I would never be that way." Beauty did not realize what came out of her mouth until it was too late, and she could not take back the words. Embarrassment started to set in until she met his eyes and he said.

"I know it would be different with you."

Beauty almost swallowed her own tongue and a long awkward silence stretched between them. Eventually, Mr. Knight turned back to the computer and Beauty sat there quietly processing what had just passed between them.

As the afternoon carried on, the easy banter returned, and it was like the awkwardness had never happened. At the end of that day, Mr. Knight engulfed Beauty in one of his amazing hugs and it lingered longer than usual. She felt his big shoulders rise and fall with his breaths. She leaned back, still in his arms and gazed up at him. He was gazing down at her and his beautiful eyes were searching hers. They gazed at each other as something unspoken passed between them. The way he was looking at her, Beauty was sure they were going to kiss. But instead, his arms dropped away and she stepped back, shaken by the intensity of her longing. With a steadying breath, she forced herself to retreat from him and back out of the room.

For the rest of the evening, Beauty obsessed over what had happened. She analyzed everything and could not decide if she had imagined it because she was projecting her feelings on to him, or if he had really meant to kiss her. Finally saying "fuck it" in her brain, she worked up the courage to start a text conversation. It was polite at first, until finally, she texted.

Beauty: Hey, it kind of felt like you wanted to kiss me.

Mr. Knight: I did.

Beauty's whole entire life changed with those two words. She felt her heart swelling and a fear creep in. She wanted Mr. Knight and he wanted her. This was such a complicated situation and she had been through so much already. She was in bed beside the sleeping Princess, contemplating what to say to Mr. Knight, when her phone rang. It was the Beast. Beauty's whole body tensed with fear. For a moment, she was afraid he might have found out what she'd been up to somehow. He could have a tracking device on her phone that monitored all her messages and calls. She would not put that kind of behavior past him. He may ignore her and the Princess for his drugs, cars, and friends, but they were still his property. He did not want them, but he would not let anyone else have them.

As Beauty answered the phone she tried not to sound nervous or suspicious.

"Hello?"

"I have to tell you something..."

The Beast sounded like he was in freak out mode. She thought, "Oh damn it, he has probably lost his job and will be around more."

"Ok, what's going on?" she said.

"I talked to my ex-stepmother today and my younger brother is in rehab because of the issues he has over what happened to him when he was a kid. She asked me to tell her the truth, so I did."

Beauty was not sure why the Beast was sounding manic over this. His little brother had been having issues with drug abuse since he was very young. She wondered what could have happened?

"Ok, what truth did you need to tell?"

The Beast did not hesitate and almost sounded proud.

"When the Drama Queen and I were younger, in our teen and pre-teen years, we had sex. Once, when my brother was five, I held him down while the Drama Queen tried to have sex with him. My ex-stepmother called me for the truth because the Drama Queen will not admit what she did or apologize for it. Apparently, there is no statute of limitations on it. I think we're the reason he's so messed up. When it happened, he told, but we said he was lying. My Dad and step-mom believed us, until today... when I confirmed and apologized to her and him for what we did to mess him up."

Beauty was speechless, trying to process

what the Beast had just told her. He could not mean what he said. That was beyond Beauty's ability to comprehend. He was talking not only of incest but child molestation. One who was the same age the Princess is now. Disgust roiled through Beauty's gut and she felt like vomiting. She might be going into shock. Her brain could not process what he said.

The Beast had been many things – abuser, monster, immature child – but Beauty had never allowed herself to think he would go so far as to hurt a child sexually. She knew he was depraved but those depravities had always been aimed at her. He liked older women, not children.

Like pieces of puzzles falling into place, his proclivities for women started to click into place. He liked short women. The Drama Queen was short, like Beauty. He wanted them to have meat on their bones to the point of what society would call obese. The Beast called them BBWs, short for Big Beautiful Women. He was always wanting Beauty to gain weight, which she hated. One minute it was gain weight and the next she was too fat. She always thought it was one of his emotional abuses, but she had never been anywhere near the size of his sister. The

Drama Queen was very obese and had very large breasts, another one of the Beast's fetish. He wanted breasts so large to be obscene. Breast, Beauty realized, just like the Drama Queen's.

The Beast always complained that Beauty's breasts were too small. Had he not used that very fact to justify his infidelity? The more Beauty thought about it and put together the pieces, she realized that the women Beast chose to watch in pornography were very similar in looks to his sister. Was the Beast in love with his vile sister? Beauty tried to wrap her head around it. Maybe she had misheard who he said his accomplice was. The Beast did grow up with several girls with his sister's name. They were all Drama Queens.

Beauty must have been silent too long because the Beast's aggravated words broke through her thoughts.

"Hello! Did you hear me? Are you still there? You better not have hung up!"

Her speech was stilted and layered in disbelief

"Sex with the Drama Queen? What do you mean?"

The Beast blew out an exasperated breath

like he was annoyed with her ignorance.

"I meant exactly what I said. When I was younger, I carried on a sexual relationship with the Drama Queen."

Still stunned and not processing the information well, Beauty asked again.

"The Drama Queen? Like your sister, the Drama Queen, or one of her friends with the same name?"

The Beast was growing more agitated. "Yes, Beauty with my sister. Jesus you are dumb."

"I'm going to be sick."

All at once Beauty felt the bile rush up her throat. She dropped the phone and rushed to the bathroom. She barely made it in time to heave up all the contents of her stomach until nothing was left. When she was finally done, she sat back against the bathroom wall and used a wash cloth to wipe her mouth. Beauty did not know how long she sat there, breathing heavily, her mind numb with the sudden realizations. She could barely process it. The woman had lived in her house. She had seen her every holiday. She recalled the jealousy she felt the Drama Queen had for her. It had started before Beauty had been pregnant with the Princess. The weird way they interacted, more like fighting lovers than siblings. The way the two of them looked at each other. Beauty had been blind to it all because the thought of something so perverted would have never crossed her mind. It was the kind of stuff people saw in movies or read about in books, not real life. At least, not in her life, but there it was all laid out in black and white. Beauty was a substitute to the Beast. Once she had the missing piece to that puzzle, Beauty knew without a doubt that the Beast's misery and problems stemmed from his longing for the one person he could not have. His own sister, the Drama Queen.

31

If you want a fairy-tale life, you have to make it yourself...

The night the Beast revealed his most vile secret, Beauty made her mind up that she would get away from the Beast and she would love who she wanted. Nothing and no one was going to stop her. She waited up that night for the Beast. When he came into the door, he seemed startled to see her sitting in the dark, at the kitchen table. The Beast had made himself vulnerable with his revelation and Beauty was going to take advantage.

"Take a seat. We need to talk."

In an un-beastly like manner, he did as he

was told. His face was guarded. Beauty felt a strength growing inside her.

"After what you told me tonight, I am going to need time to process all of it. I do not want you to touch me. I do not want to be around you or your sister for the holidays. I am not comfortable with it. I cannot let you be alone with the Princess at all, and I do not want her around your sister either. What you two did was incest and molestation. As you stated, there is no statute of limitations on that crime. I will not say a word to anyone about what you told me if you give me the space I am asking for. In fact, I think you need to deal with that situation. Since you're spending most weekends near your sister's home when you're car racing, maybe it would be best if you slept at her house or in one of your friend's houses until I can come to terms with this. You are always going on about how much you miss being close to your family. I understand now why this has always been such a problem for you, and why you have such a need to be near your sister."

Beauty met his eyes on that last statement and held her ground. She was telling him in so many words that she knew exactly how twisted the love in his heart was. The Beast did not try to argue or deny any of it. Instead, he smiled and nodded, as if he agreed that it was the best idea in the world. Beauty felt even more disgust for the Beast.

"Until I come to terms with this, I would like you to sleep in the guest bedroom when you are home."

A sliver of malice crossed the Beast's eyes, a protest on his lips. Beauty held up a hand.

"On this, I will not be moved. The Princess will either sleep with me or at my parents. You will not be alone with her. Again, I remind you that there is no statute of limitations on what you two did, so I took precautions and emailed all the information to the Queen. If you do not respect my wishes or anything happens to me, she will notify the authorities. Since you and I know you will never leave or let us go without it ending in one of our deaths, this is the only option on the table."

Beauty could tell the Beast was pissed, but she put on her bravest face and stood her ground, meeting his glare and refusing to be the first one to turn away. Everything she had said to the Beast about this being the only option was bullshit. She was taking herself and the Princess away from him. She needed a place he knew nothing about and protection. When she made her move, she and the Princess would disappear, and the Beast would never see them again.

Finally, the Beast looked away and nodded.

"Ok, we will do it your way for a while."

Beauty did not miss the caveat he placed at the end, but she rose from the table and moved to walk past him. He reached out and grabbed her wrist, stopping her in her tracks. He had not grabbed her like that in almost two years. She glared down at him.

"Take your hand off me."

His grip briefly tightened and then released.

The Beast said nothing, and Beauty went straight to her bedroom, locked the door and propped a chair under it. In the darkness, she finally let herself feel the old familiar fear. She was shaking from the encounter as she crawled into bed. A sense of dread crept into Beauty as she realized what she had done. Her cell phone was clutched in one hand, ready to dial for help if it was needed. She knew a storm was coming and the next moves she made would be the most important in her and the Princess's lives.

Beauty heard the Beast leave. He never went to

sleep in the guest bedroom. It was the weekend, so she hoped he had opted to go to his sister's or a friend in the early morning hours. Beauty waited in the silent darkness for his return, but it never came. As the first rays of sunlight began to peak through the curtains, Beauty stared at her daughter's angelic little face. A new resolve had set in and she was going to get them away from the monster's clutches. She tried not to let grotesque images of the Beast and his sister together invade her thoughts. Her life was like a bad lifetime movie and it was up to her to make sure that the Princess never suffered as she had. Her cell phone vibrated in her hand as a text came through.

The Beast: I made it to my sister's. I love you. We will get through this.

Beauty stuck the phone under her pillow and rolled her eyes in disgust. "Nope, we sure won't, sister fucker."

This was the proverbial straw that broke the camel's back. Her phone vibrated again. Beauty sighed in frustration, figuring it would be one of the Beast's attempts to play at a honeymoon phase. But a wide grin spread across Beauty's face as she saw who it was from.

Mr. Knight: Good morning, beautiful. How

are you today?

Beauty knew he was married, but their connection was undeniable, and she had decided to go with it. She knew if the Beast ever found out, he would kill her, but she hoped that by that time, she and the Princess would be long gone and safe. Beauty was playing a deadly game, but it was one she was determined to win.

Beauty: Good morning, handsome. I am good, thank you for asking. How are you doing?

His response was immediate.

Mr. Knight: I'm good, just thinking about you.

Beauty's smile was so wide her cheeks hurt. Her mood did an immediate one eighty. By the time the Princess woke, Beauty and Mr. Knight had texted back and forth several times. He made her feel at peace even with just texts.

That weekend, she spent quality time with her daughter and talked to Mr. Knight. It was the best weekend she had ever had. Even the Beast's occasional half-hearted manipulative texts did not bring down her mood. By Monday morning, she felt like a new woman. She would not be seeing Mr. Knight because she had training starting at her old office, but she did have to pass by the new office on the way.

Her new trainer was a stern and unyielding woman. She was like the scary teacher from school. Beauty was only able to check her messages on breaks but was always ecstatic to see several from Mr. Knight. He was always thinking about her and saying he missed her. Beauty was trying to go slow and be cautious after the way the Beast had played her in the beginning, but she was no longer the naïve girl she had been years before. Beauty had learned a lot from the Beast and had developed a sense for when people were genuine and when they weren't. Mr. Knight was nothing like the Beast and Beauty had never met a more honest person. He did not have the manipulation gene. He was so honest that against Beauty's advice, he had told his wife he wanted a divorce and she needed to move out. The woman had not taken it well and was refusing to budge from the house. She was also making his life a living hell. But he could not lie and wanted to pursue the connection he and Beauty felt.

At the end of that first day of training, Beauty was exhausted, but she stopped by the office anyway to see Mr. Knight. His truck was the only vehicle in the parking lot. Everyone else was gone for the day which meant they would be alone in the office. Beauty's pulse began to race. She just wanted one of his reassuring hugs and to smell his soothing scent. Nothing more. That's what she told herself until she saw him. He looked so good in khaki pants and the favorite hoodie he had bought while deployed overseas. The minute they saw each other, they were both smiling like kids in a candy store, and Beauty impulsively began to run toward him. With arms outstretched, she jumped up into his embrace and he picked her up like she weighed nothing. Instinctively, Beauty wrapped her legs around his waist and leaned her head into his. The kiss that followed surprised them both and was a little awkward at first. But as his warm lip pressed against hers and began to move, Beauty melted into it, letting go of all the apprehension and fear she felt. It was a kiss for the record books, like something out of the ending of a romance novel or movie.

When they finely pulled apart and stared into each other's eyes, they were both breathing heavily. Mr. Knight had a shy grin on his face and Beauty was flushed all over. His grin widened, and it made Beauty giggle like a child. At some point, she had wrapped her arms around his neck and was holding him close. He leaned his forehead into hers

"Well... that was…"

"Yeah, I know," she replied between breaths.

They stayed silent for a few moments, soaking up each other and the magnitude of the kiss. It held so many promises and so many complications, but in Beauty's mind, it was worth it. She had never felt true love and she thought maybe, just maybe... if it did exist... this man could be hers.

Finally, Beauty reluctantly pulled back a little and looked from one side of the ground to the other, then met Mr. Knight's eyes and giggled again.

"I have never been picked up like that before. Am I hurting you?"

He nuzzled his nose against hers and whispered into her lips. "Never, you weigh nothing."

Beauty blushed. "I guess you better put me down. It is already getting late."

Mr. Knight briefly squeezed her tighter, then Beauty unwrapped her legs from around his waist and slid down his body. A sexy growl escaped his lips. She was silent as she stepped away and turned her back to him. On impulse, she threw a sexy smile over her shoulder in his direction and he gave her one in return.

"You headed my way?" she asked as she threw a little extra sway into her hips.

Mr. Knight quickly grabbed his stuff and followed her to the parking lot, opening all the doors like the gentleman he was. Beauty was on cloud nine. Mr. Knight escorted her to her car, opened her door and gave her a quick peck on the lips. Then, he hopped in his truck and signaled for her to go ahead. He called her as they drove in the same direction to their separate homes, with separate lives, and partners neither of them wanted. Beauty laughed and felt giddy as they talked. Beauty knew without a doubt that after that kiss, if she could pull this off, this man would be her future. If she didn't, he could also mean her death.

32

She looked so good In Love...

Beauty had a new lease on life and was more determined than ever to make a fresh start. She wanted to leave the Beast in the dust and his indifference toward her made her believe she could. Beauty knew she still had to take precautions to be safe. The Beast was unpredictable, but one thing she knew for sure... he would never let another man be a father to his child, even if he was no kind of father at all.

The more time she spent with Mr. Knight, the stronger their bond grew. Beauty was falling head over heels in love with the man while trying to keep it a secret from the world. She did her best, but she could not hide the glow of happiness around her. Jasmine had noticed and became Beauty's confidant. It felt good to have a female friend to confide in after so many years of being isolated. Beauty loved the fact that she was starting to feel like her old self.

One evening, she went to pick up the Princess from the Queen's and her mother gave her the strangest look.

"What's up with you? Who is he?"

Beauty's eyes grew wide as she tried to stutter out an excuse.

The Queen gave Beauty an incredulous look. Her mother knew her to well.

"Fine, it's a guy I work with. He is tall, dark haired, blue eyed, handsome, hardworking, kind, sweet, generous, loving, and muscled. The list could go on Mom, but basically he is everything I could have ever hoped for or dreamed of."

The Queen threw her arms around Beauty and hugged her tightly.

"Thank GOD! I knew if anyone worth anything paid any attention to you, and you actually noticed, you would finally kick that piece of shit to the curb."

Beauty leaned back from her mom and met her eyes. "He's married and it's complicated."

The Queen scoffed at Beauty. "Oh honey, no woman is a match for my Beauty. You got this."

Beauty just stared at her mother for a moment. "Are you telling me to go after him and take him? He is married, Mama, and she is a female version of the Beast in Troll form."

The Queen raised her eyebrows at Beauty and smirked. "If you want him, then go get him. The only person stopping you is you."

Beauty thought about that then said, "How did you know?"

The Queen smiled a gorgeous smile at Beauty. "Because my baby has not looked this good or this happy in a long time. You're starting to look like your old self."

Beauty was proud her mother thought she looked good. It had been a long time since she had felt her mother thought anything good about her.

"Thank you, Mama, but I am worried. This is a very dangerous game I'm playing."

Beauty looked her mother in the eyes and tried to convey just how dangerous the situation was.

The Queen patted Beauty's back. "Don't worry baby. Everything is going to be ok."

Beauty hoped her mother was right.

The holidays were fast approaching, and Beauty opted not to go anywhere near the Beast's family. She could barely stomach the thought of the Drama Queen let alone suffer through having to be in the same room with her. That family was such a twisted screwed-up lot, that Beauty could not even imagine in her wildest dreams the stuff they came up with. Everything was a competition with them and they were all a few bricks shy of a full load.

Mr. Knight was going to be gone for two weeks between Christmas and the New Year and neither of them could stand the thought of being away from each other for that long. The nights and weekends had become so hard that Mr. Knight and Beauty had started finding reasons to slip away and meet for minutes, just to steal a quick kiss or hug. They were like addicts needing a fix in the honeymoon stage of the relationship. Things at Mr. Knight's home were rough, and he was dealing with a lot from the Troll. She was being insufferable and refusing to leave. She even implemented the help of family and friends, anyone she could get to try and talk him out of the divorce. She went as far as to hold an intervention with her parents and best friends, where they spent the whole time berating him and trying to convince him he had Post Traumatic Stress Disorder from his deployments, and the "affair" was the result of his condition.

Beauty was so glad that Mr. Knight held fast to his convictions and feelings for her. She knew she was not the complete reason for his decision to divorce the Troll, but she had been the catalyst. Her presence, before anything had happened between them, had shown Mr. Knight how unhappy he truly was.

On Beauty's home front, things were much the same. The Beast was distant, withdrawn, but she rarely had to see him. Beauty was glad for this, but the lack of attention made Beauty bolder and she took more risks. Maybe subconsciously, she wanted to get caught because it was getting increasingly hard to keep her secret and maintain separate lives.

Beauty had devised a plan to see Mr. Knight while he was away. She arranged for the Queen to watch the Princess and told the Beast she had to go out of town for work. Without getting into specifics, she said she had to attend training for her new position. This was a believable lie because Beauty had months of training ahead of her. The job required her to be gone for weeks at a time until training was finished. The Beast did not question Beauty. He rarely questioned Beauty anymore. He did his thing and she did hers. This lack of care for what she did led Beauty to believe the Beast trusted her, which was a mistake on her part.

The trip allowed Beauty to spend time with Mr. Knight, away from all the worries she had daily. But she was still nervous the entire time. She feared the Beast would find out, but Beauty had made up her mind. Mr. Knight was the man she wanted to be with. The trip only solidified that fact.

When Beauty arrived, she rushed into Mr. Knight's arms and leapt into his embrace. She had become accustomed to this greeting. He would lift her up and kiss her passionately. The heat and longing grew to a point where it threatened to bubble over. Beauty knew what this trip meant. They would be staying together in the same bed and would not resist each other any longer. They would be taking the next step.

Beauty was nervous because she had not

been with anyone but the Beast in years, and only knew his version of sex... which was brutal. There was no passionate love making or gentle caresses for Beauty. She should have shied away from a man's touch after all the trauma she had endured, but not with Mr. Knight. His touch made her feel safe, beautiful, and loved. With every caress or look, she could see that this man cherished her.

Mr. Knight was staying on base in a studio apartment room. There was a small living area, kitchen, bathroom, and bedroom. Beauty was nervous when they first entered, and she took in her surroundings. This would be the place where her life would forever change. Once she took this step, there would be no going back.

Mr. Knight set her bags down and gave her one of his gorgeous smiles.

"Would you like anything to eat or drink?"

Beauty shook her head and peered up at him through her dark lashes. He was so sexy it was taking her breath away. Mr. Knight responded with one of his own looks. He was like a predator ready to devour his prey. Beauty felt her heart skip a beat. With one swift movement, Mr. Knight had scooped her up. Beauty wrapped her legs around his waist as they kissed each other as if their lives depended on it. The emotions and passion were so intense Beauty could feel herself growing more aroused than she had ever been. Mr. Knight moved them through the small apartment and into the bedroom, kissing Beauty, the entire way. Her head was spinning with the delicious arousal and scent of him. His mouth was warm on her skin as he kissed a trail across her cheek to her ear lobe and down her neck. She let out a tiny gasp and moaned as he moved his way back to her mouth. He was such a strong, powerful man that he made Beauty feel tiny in comparison. His large hand cupped and kneaded her ass as she pulled him in for a deeper kiss. His dark hair was soft under Beauty's fingers. With a boldness she never though was in her, she tugged his head back. This man made her feel confident and powerful as a woman. She desperately tried to tug his shirt off while still in his muscled arms, and when the shirt would not budge, she let out a frustrated groan.

Between kisses, she demanded, "This... off... now." Her brain hummed, "Whoa, where had that inner vixen come from?"

Mr. Knight gave her a sly smile against her lips and finally placed her on her feet.

"Yes, ma'am."

Beauty watched in fascination as he kicked off his shoes and slipped off his socks. Damn, he even had pretty feet for a man. His nimble fingers clasped the hem of the threadbare t-shirt he was wearing, and with confident ease, he pulled it over his head. Her mouth gaped open. The man was a God. Standing there, shirtless, with low slung jeans and bare feet, he looked like something out of a modeling campaign.

Beauty took a moment to drink in the tanned and toned skin. He had a large and beautiful Phoenix tattoo along one side of his ribcage, and a mural of St. Michael along the other. Both broad shoulders and biceps were adorned with dark ink one tattoo, drifting over and covering his pectoral muscle. Beauty studied one of his tattoos and realized it was the Grim Reaper. As her eyes drifted lower to the v-cuts he sported, her breath hitched. The man had v's for fuck's sake. She was such a goner.

Beauty forced her embarrassment to the back of her mind and looked below the yummy abs and v's. There was a very large, very noticeable bulge, barely being contained by the low-slung jeans and her body gave an inner shake. Grim Reaper indeed. This man might be the death of her. His eyes heated the longer she stared. His hands moved toward the fly of his jeans and he raised his eyebrows with a sly smile as if asking her silently, "Should I continue?" Beauty gulped and nodded, her mouthwatering at the sight of him.

Mr. Knight made slow and deliberate movements as he started to unbutton his jeans. Beauty's eyes were transfixed. The jeans slid down his powerful thighs and lean calves to pool at his feet. He hooked a thumb on either side of his boxer briefs and winked at Beauty. She could feel the flush all over her body and motioned for him to continue. With that sly smile still in place, he shimmied out of the briefs and jeans. What sprang forth was almost overwhelming. Mr. Knight was big everywhere!

Her gaze started at his handsome face and roamed all the way down to his feet. With a bold move, she did a twirling motion with one finger as if to say, "Spin for me, darlin!" Mr. Knight chuckled a little and spun around with his back facing her. His back was corded and toned, the tattoo's covering his shoulder blades and sides. Her gaze roamed down and good God, she saw the best ass she had ever seen on a man. It was better than any she had ever seen in the movies.

The damn man was perfect, and Beauty began to feel self-conscious about her own body. She was not skinny, but she wasn't flabby either – she was curvy. She had given birth to a baby, so her stomach would never be as toned as it had once been. He breasts were a small B-cup, but she knew she had a great ass, so she at least had that going for her. Beauty's gaze was still on his ass when Mr. Knight turned around. Her eyes were instantly drawn to his huge erection. Beauty had never been with a man that size and worried he wouldn't fit. Mr. Knights eyes were hungry.

"My turn."

Beauty stilled even more as he approached and motioned for her to lift her arms. He gently pulled her shirt over her head and unclasped her bra. Out of pure instinct, she lowered her eyes and crossed her arms over her breasts. Mr. Knight placed a finger under her chin and brought her eyes up to his.

"You are so beautiful." Then, he gently kissed her lips. It was a soft kiss, merely a brush, and Beauty relaxed a little. He grazed warm fingertips down her abdomen, to her belly button. Beauty shivered from his touch. He knelt before her in all his naked glory and brushed light kisses just below her belly button.

Beauty dropped her arms from her breast to run her fingers through that soft hair of his. With nimble fingers, he unclasped her jeans and slid them off her. He placed a hand on either side of her hips and sat back to gaze at her. Beauty felt a rush of self-consciousness and moved to cover her breasts again. Mr. Knight stopped her with gentle hands and shook his head from side to side.

"No, you are the most gorgeous woman I have ever seen. Never cover yourself around me."

Beauty blushed. "You don't have to say that."

Mr. Knight locked eyes with her and said, "If it wasn't the truth, I would not say it. I wish you could see yourself through my eyes."

Beauty felt her heart pounding with pride at his words and look. His eyes were filled with such sincerity that Beauty felt overwhelmed with emotions. She was standing almost completely naked in front of a God of a man and he found her beautiful. She had not felt this loved or beautiful in her entire life.

Mr. Knight ran a fingertip along the lace of her panties and began to push them down her hips. When she had kicked them off, he buried his face in her center and took long, deep breaths. A growl or moan escaped him.

"You smell so good. I need to taste you."

Before Beauty could answer, he had scooped her up and had her legs spread wide as he began to hungrily lick and suck at her most intimate of places. Beauty's back arched with the pleasure. He was the kind of guy who excelled at everything he did, and this was no exception. The tingle started in her spine and spread throughout her whole body. With an explosion of sensation, she felt the orgasm to her toes and her whole body quaked. She yelled out his name and moaned with the force of it. Mr. Knight brought his long, muscled arms up and began to play with her nipples. Beauty was a ball of nerve-endings and sensation. She had never felt anything so good in her life. His warm hot tongue continued to lap at her core between sensual sucks at her bud and kisses. It all felt good. Too good... so good it almost hurt.

She tried to crawl away, but he was having none of it. He held her in place as he treated her like an all-you-can-eat buffet, and before Beauty could catch her breath, she was gripping the sheets and crying out as another orgasm overtook her. She felt like he did this for hours.

By the time he finally lifted his head, Beauty's legs were quivering, and she had lost count of the orgasms. He crawled up her body and placed a strong arm on either side of her head. Her legs were spread wide as he nestled his large cock into her. The head probed her entrance. It felt hot and pulsed against her slick folds. He held her eyes, lips glistening with her many releases. He licked them, and Beauty moaned. He slowly lowered his mouth to hers and entered her at the same time. The kiss was passionate and gentle, and she began to feel a fullness and pressure as he inched into her so slowly it almost felt like torture. Beauty could not handle it and with one swift move, gripped his ass and plunged him deep into her core. The head immediately hit her sensitive sweet spot and Beauty's insides clenched around him as she orgasmed again, and then he started to move. His voice was guttural and feral.

Through clenched teeth, he gritted out, "God, you are so tight."

Beauty couldn't speak at this point, she was all moans and on the verge of speaking in tongues. With each thrust and slide, she could feel her orgasm building again. Was it possible to die from this many orgasms? She did not know, but God, it felt heavenly. He moved his powerful arms under her and the move widened her legs. As he gripped her ass, her hips and back arched into a position that allowed him even deeper access. His pace and thrusts quickened. She could feel him getting closer to his own release as he grew impossibly bigger inside her. Beauty could feel herself about to tumble over the edge of bliss again, when he let out the sexiest moan she had ever heard. Pushing her right over the edge, he emptied his hot seed inside her. This only intensified her release and his whole body trembled as his orgasm went on and on until he was twitching and unhurriedly thrusting into her. The room was quiet... the only sound their breaths.

They laid like that with him inside her and her holding him close for what could have been minutes or hours. When both of their breaths had steadied and the sweat on their bodies began to cool, Mr. Knight looked at Beauty with eyes full of emotion.

"I love you."

Beauty's answer was immediate and without thought.

"I love you too."

Mr. Knight grinned so widely it made Beauty smile in return. He leaned in and kissed her with all the love he felt. Soon, they were making love again and Beauty was lost in the bliss of their passion.

It was not until many hours later, as she lay exhausted and content, wrapped in his warm strong arms, that the magnitude of their love-making hit her. It had been the most mind-blowing experience of her life and she would forever be changed by it. She could not go the rest of her life without this man in it. At that moment, she wished time would stop if only for a little while, so she could feel that happiness for just a bit longer. Mr. Knight's soft, steady breaths started to lull her to sleep, and for the first time in a very long time, Beauty fell into a deep and nightmare-free sleep.

33

It's not all smooth sailing from here...

That trip to see Mr. Knight had changed Beauty. Colors seemed brighter. Happiness more possible. A few weeks after he returned from his trip, Beauty decided to let him meet the Princess. He had been asking about the little girl for months, but Beauty did not want to go there until she was sure Mr. Knight was their future.

So, one weekend, while the Beast was supposed to be off at his vile sister's, Beauty invited Mr. Knight to the park for a play date with her and the Princess. Beauty told the Princess they would be going to the park with her friend from work. Mr. Knight and Beauty had already agreed that in front of the Princess, everything would be strictly platonic. Neither of them wanted to confuse or cause the Princess issues.

When the day finally came, Beauty and the Princess were playing at the park when they heard the rumble of an engine. Like the Knight in Shining Armor he was, Mr. Knight rolled up on a slick, shiny motorcycle in all his gear. The Princess was in awe as she watched Mr. Knight dismount and remove his helmet, jacket, and gloves. She tugged at Beauty's sleeve and whispered.

"Is that our friend, Mommy?"

Beauty grinned at her daughter's use of ours, not hers. She could tell that Mr. Knight had already made an impression on the Princess, just like the first time Beauty saw him.

Mr. Knight walked toward them with an easy step, his eyes zeroing in on the little girl. She had his full attention and he was as enamored with her as she was with him. The Princess craned her head up and looked into his beautiful blue eyes. A wide grin spread across his face and the Princess giggled.

"Hi." Her little smile and wave was adorable.

"Hi, you must be the little Princess I've heard so much about. Nice to meet you!" He held out a hand, but just like her mommy, she jumped into his strong arms.

"Wanna go swing?"

Mr. Knight nodded and off the two went.

Beauty marveled at their instant bond. The Princess had never responded to the Beast like she did to Mr. Knight. The two were like peas in a pod.

Beauty sat back and watched as the two played.

When Mr. Knight approached her, and the Princess was out of hearing distance, he said, "I love her."

Beauty smiled. "I'm glad to hear it. I love her too. She's an awesome kid, my little mini-me."

Mr. Knight looked at Beauty and with a very serious tone, he said, "No, I mean I love her. Not like, 'oh I love her, she's a great kid.' I mean like the instant I saw her, everything that had been missing in my life clicked into place. I have always felt like I was searching for something and pieces of me were missing. When I met you, a piece clicked into place. Now that

I've met her, there was another click and suddenly that 'missing' feeling was gone. My puzzle is complete. You two are it for me. Y'all are my family. Y'all are the future I want. I love you. Both of you. I want to be a father to that little girl because she needs one. A real one. That is what she deserves and what you deserve."

Beauty was taken aback and speechless at his declaration. No one had ever been so sincere or said such things to her. Not even the Beast when he was playing at manipulation. She was overwhelmed but needed time to process what he said. She gazed past him and smiled at the Princess as she played. Then, she looked back at Mr. Knight and met his eyes. She had not thought it out. She did not over-analyze it. She just spoke from the heart with the words that felt right.

"Ok, if that is what you really want, and you are all in. I will be all in to. I love you, I have been waiting for you all my life. But, you must understand, I will always put her first. I want what is best for my daughter, and I can see no one else being a better male role model than you. I trust you with her and I cannot even trust her biological father with her. So, that says a lot about how I feel about you."

That day proved to be another milestone for Beauty, the Princess, and Mr. Knight. However, it was not all meant to be hearts and flowers. Their situations were very complicated, and Mr. Knight had his own living hell at home with the Troll, and Beauty could tell it was starting to take its toll on him. She wished the woman would just have some dignity and leave, but she also felt guilty for wanting that. Beauty had never intended to break up his marriage and knew it had been on the downswing, headed toward divorce, even before she came along. But still, she felt guilt.

The Troll would text Mr. Knight several times a day and call Beauty the "hoebag" or "homewrecker." This hurt, but how was she to deny it. She had not meant to fall in love with Mr. Knight. It had happened and felt like the hand of fate. Beauty knew of the concept of soulmates, but she had never truly believed in it until Mr. Knight came along. The connection had been instant and very real, like they had known each other all their lives.

Beauty started to really worry for Mr. Knight when the Troll became increasingly unstable with each passing day. She was refusing to leave his house. It was his, but the Troll was determined to punish Mr. Knight for daring to divorce her and force him into staying with her or lose his childhood home and land. Mr. Knight would never lay a hand on a woman in violence, and the Troll knew this, so she herself started becoming violent.

In one incident, she cornered Mr. Knight with a knife and tried to stab him. Another time, she tried to run him over with the truck. She started monitoring all his texts, emails, and phone calls. She even followed him on a few occasions. Beauty understood living with madness, but she also knew that if Mr. Knight abandoned the property, the Troll would get it, and she knew how his family home was important to him.

She tried to be there for him and eventually, their bond grew as they shared stories of the troubles at home. Beauty divulged some of the Beast's past actions and Mr. Knight immediately wanted to get Beauty and the Princess out of his presence. They decided that the only truly safe place for Beauty and the Princess to flee to was to his home. Mr. Knight did not care anymore about trying to appease the Troll out of guilt. He wanted her gone and finally consulted a lawyer.

Beauty had known it would come to that. The Troll was determined to keep Mr. Knight and continue enjoying the life he gave her. But, Mr. Knight was the kind of man who needed to come to conclusions himself, so that is what Beauty let him do. He had tried to do things amicably and talk the Troll into leaving. He had a naïve notion or hope that she'd go away quietly, but Beauty had known. Madness and obsession were two emotions the Beast had made Beauty all too familiar with. Another trait of Mr. Knight that Beauty discovered was that once he had made up his mind, there was no swaying him from his decision.

Somewhere along the way, amid all the madness, Mr. Knight had chosen Beauty and the Princess, and to him there could be no going back.

Beauty was relieved and happy that he felt the way he did, but she was still stuck with the Beast until he could get the Troll out of the house. At this point, it had been months and she was still refusing to go. Mr. Knight was getting ready to file for divorce and force her out, when she pulled a fast one and served him with papers. Because the Troll served him, he was barred from going to his family home and was virtually homeless. Thankfully, the Queen had an apartment she could let him stay in. So, Mr. Knight moved into the apartment and shortly thereafter, so did Beauty and the Princess.

The Beast had spent so much time at his sister's, he started living there. The Princess and Beauty rarely saw him, and Beauty lived a quiet life with Mr. Knight. The Beast did not even come to help when she moved all the stuff out of the house. Nor did he question her actions. His attitude was so indifferent that Beauty started to let her guard down. Maybe her mind would not let her remember that when she had tried to leave before, the Beast had forced his way back in. Beauty was not stupid enough to clue the Beast into Mr. Knight's existence or the fact that they were living together. As far as the Beast knew, she and the Princess lived with the Queen, and he got to live his life doing whatever he wanted, whenever he wanted, with no attachments. He did not even offer financial support. He did not show any interest in Beauty or the Princess. That should have been Beauty's first clue that something was off with the whole situation.

This was the Beast she was dealing with. He could lie in wait for prolonged periods of times and strike without warning. Beauty foolishly dropped her guard because of his indifference and the Beast probably would have stayed indifferent had the Troll not decided that she needed to have a talk with the Beast.

The vengeful woman blamed Beauty for the destruction of her marriage, even though it had been over long before Beauty came along. But like most spoiled narcissists, she could not take responsibility for her own actions or lack thereof. It was not enough that she was keeping Mr. Knight's rightful home. Instead of trying to focus on making her own new life, she found out who the Beast was and contacted him through social media. Then, she told him everything she knew and purposefully set a monster after Beauty and the Princess. The hateful woman sealed Beauty's death warrant with one phone conversation.

34

She had it coming...

Summer had just begun, and the days slowly turned into the sweltering heat only the South could supply. Beauty had a plan in motion. She and the Princess were going to disappear from the Beast's life.

It was the Friday before Father's Day weekend. Knight had managed to get his property back for a brief time, and Beauty was tired of living her double life. She let the Beast believe that she and the Princess would be joining him at his vile sister's for the holiday. Instead, they would hide at Knight's property.

That evening, she turned off her cell phone,

packed their bags, and tried not to look back. The entire time, Beauty had an overwhelming sense of dread and anxiety, but she tried to put on a happy face for the Princess and Knight. The weekend started off well enough. The bond between her Knight and her daughter had grown so much that no one would've known he was not her biological father. There was a pure untainted love between the two. The Princess had Knight wrapped around her little finger and she thought the man hung the moon. It made Beauty's heart swell every time she saw the love between them. Her daughter had never known a truly loving man until Knight came into the picture.

Friday evening went well, and Beauty never turned her cell phone on. Saturday started out relaxing and anyone on the outside looking in on the three of them would think they looked like a happy little family. Then, Knight's cell phone began to ring. It was the Queen calling.

"Beauty needs to call the police and explain the situation, right now."

Beauty stared at the phone, perplexed.

"The police? Why?"

She could hear the urgency in her mother's

voice.

"That idiot called the police and reported you and the Princess missing. He has been blowing up our phones, acting a fool and making threats."

Beauty could feel all the blood drain from her face. Her voice was barely audible when she spoke, "Yes, ma'am, I will do that right now."

Her hands were shaking as she dialed the number for the local law enforcement. The police had never helped Beauty before. When the dispatcher answered, and Beauty gave her name, she was immediately directed to an officer in charge of handling the report. He was kind to Beauty as she explained the situation. He even offered to help Beauty by calling the Beast and letting him know they were safe, but the relationship was over, and he was not to contact her. When the conversation was done, Beauty felt a modicum of relief, but she still could not shake that feeling of dread.

The situation with Knight's property was only temporary and she still had to work. Knight assured Beauty he would protect her and the Princess, but she knew that he had no real idea of what the Beast was truly capable of. Beauty prayed the Beast would let her go and she could really start a new life this time.

By Monday morning, Beauty was on a razor's edge. She had to go to work and knew without a doubt the Beast would be waiting for her. When she had finally turned on her cell phone, the night before, she had received hundreds of missed calls, texts, and her voicemail was full. The messages flip flopped between pleading and threatening. The most telling of the messages were the ones where the Beast told her he had spoken with the Troll and knew all the secrets Beauty had been keeping. Beauty contemplated calling in sick to work, but she did not want to be home alone and risk the Beast catching her there.

That day, Beauty had chosen to carpool with Knight for her safety. She tried to work and focus on the tasks in front of her, but the growing fear inside her was becoming crippling. Then, she heard a familiar sound. It was an engine revving. The hairs on her arms stood up and a chill went down her spine. It was the Beast's car. Beauty got up from her desk and went to her tiny sliver of a window. The Beast was parked just outside, staring at her. She did not want a scene at work. Beauty needed her job and could not afford to lose it. She knew the Beast would do whatever it took to get her attention, even if that action cost her the job she needed so badly. With her whole body shaking, she made her way outside, but stopped where she could still be seen by the people in the lobby. The Beast exited his car and approached her. With each step he took, she had to will her feet to stay rooted, so she would not run. Beauty could see the rage boiling just beneath the surface. This was not the detached Beast of the last few years. The monster walking toward her was the one she feared more than anything. He was the Beast of the past. A violent animal ready to rip her to shreds. He was only steps away when her resolve gave way to fear and she bolted back into the building. Her heart was pounding so loudly she could barely hear the screaming going on around her.

Beauty crumpled into the nearest old vinyl chair in the lobby. She could see the chaos taking place outside. Knight must have been alerted to the Beast's presence and had headed outside to confront him. Ever the cool and calm soldier, he stood towering over the Beast with arms crossed. It was a menacing stance that made the Beast stand back from him. One of the women she worked with was speaking to her, but she registered none of it. Beauty only had eyes for the two men she could see through the grimy glass. The Beast was screaming and cursing at Knight, but none of the insanity seemed to faze him. He stood like a stone guard barring the Beast from entering the building. Beauty could sense the Beast's cruel intentions. It all felt surreal to her. Watching the man she now loved standing guard against the monster she had feared for so many years. The Beast was acting like a raving lunatic until the police cars pulled up. Beauty watched with no surprise as the Beast morphed into the normal, calm, victim mask he liked to portray around authority. She could barely hear the conversation between the men and only caught snippets. But from what she could discern, the Beast was doing his best to spin a tale where he was the victim. He told the officers that his wife was "cheating" on him with Knight. Disgust dripped from the Beast every time he used the man's name or looked in his direction. Still, Knight stood tall with no shame or remorse. The officer separated Knight and the Beast calmly, getting each side of the men's stories. When it was all over, one of the officers patted Knight on the arm and he headed inside.

Beauty watched as the officer went over to the Beast and clearly instructed him to leave. As the Beast scowled and turned, Beauty let out a sigh of relief. Until the Beast looked back and shot Beauty a killing look. She knew what that one look meant. He was telling her "this isn't over," Knight sat down beside Beauty and wrapped a strong arm around her shoulders. She was audibly shaking and barely keeping the tears stinging her eyes from falling.

"It's ok, baby. Shhhh, it's ok. He isn't coming back. I told you I would protect you."

Beauty let the tears spill then, because she knew it was not going to be ok. Nothing was ever going to be ok and no one, not even Knight, could protect her."

The officer approached them.

"Ma'am, I have instructed your husband not to return to these premises again. We will be putting this building on close patrol and if he is caught here, he will be arrested."

Beauty nodded her acknowledgment and mustered a whispered thank you.

The tears had slowed to mere trickles from the corners of her eyes. Embarrassment started to set in, as she looked around the room and saw everyone staring.

Knight whispered in her ear and squeezed her shoulder.

"I will be right back. I promise I am not going far."

He rose and escorted the officer to the double glass doors. Beauty peered at them through glassy eyes. Their conversation was muffled but ended in a handshake. Then, the officer was out the door and Knight was back at her side with his strong safe arms wrapped around her. She leaned her tear stained face into his chest and took a long deep breath of his calming scent. They stayed there in silence for a long time; her hiccupping from her crying fit, and he, rubbing circles on her back as he made soothing sounds.

Eventually, everyone around them went back to what they had been doing before the confrontation. Beauty did not want to see any of the pitying glances or hear their whispers. She just wanted to run far away from all of it. A bone deep feeling of exhaustion started to set in. Her voice was a murmur as she spoke into Knight's ear.

"Please take me home."

He ran a warm hand down her hair and gently caressed her cheek.

"Whatever you need, baby. Stay here and I will take care of everything."

When he rose, Beauty immediately felt the absence of his embrace and felt a weary chill. With each moment he was gone, her anxiety ramped up. She was a sitting duck. What if the Beast did not care about the police warnings? What if he was sitting in a nearby parking lot, waiting and watching for her to be alone. She began to fidget and look around nervously. It must have drawn the attention of one of the ladies in the lobby, because she came over and placed a soft wrinkled hand on Beauty's trembling ones.

"Are you ok, honey? Do you need anything?"

Beauty gazed up at the stranger. She was a sweet elderly woman with a flair for color. She was decked out in a menagerie of reds, golds, and oranges, her hair a wild, silvery mess sticking out in all directions. She looked like an eccentric patchwork quilt and Beauty could not shake the sense that she knew the woman. The lady felt familiar, like a favorite childhood blanket or worn jeans. In all the chaos, Beauty had never seen the woman come in. Had she been there the whole time? Beauty shuddered at the thought of this sweet lady witnessing such an embarrassment. Thankfully, when Beauty met the woman's eyes, she found they showed no pity, only sympathy. Beauty managed a small smile.

"No, Ma'am. Thank you though."

The woman sat down beside her and kept her hand clasped over Beauty's. She patted them lightly as she spoke.

"If you don't mind, I think I will rest here a minute."

Beauty felt a rush of gratitude to the stranger.

"Thank you, Ma'am, I would appreciate the company. But I don't think I will be much for polite conversation."

The sweet, little Fairy Godmother of a woman just kept patting and smiling. Beauty almost missed the wink the woman gave her.

"That's fine with me, dearie. Silence isn't always a terrible thing. Sometimes silence can be your best friend when you really need it."

Beauty nodded and bowed her head, studying her shoes and the floor. The two women sat in that bubble of silence until Knight returned. As he approached, the little woman rose and placed a finger under Beauty's chin, lifting it until their eyes met.

"This may all feel like the world is about to end, and I can see them troubles are weighing on you hard. Just remember, no matter what you face, in the end, it's all going to work out just fine."

Beauty stared after the woman as she pivoted far too quickly for someone her age and headed out the doors, disappearing around the corner of the building. Knight placed an arm around Beauty and helped her to her feet.

"Who was that?"

Beauty just shook her head, still confused by the woman and her parting words.

"I don't know... but she was nice. Have you ever seen her before?"

Knight furrowed his brows as if searching his brain. "No, I don't think I have, but she seemed so familiar."

Now they were both staring at the spot where she had disappeared. Beauty leaned into Knight's strong and warm body. Tucked under his shoulder was the only time she felt remotely safe. Her voice had a faraway cast to it.

"I felt the same way, but I know I've never seen her before."

Knight looked down at her with pure love

and protection in his eyes. "Let's go home, baby. We have had enough excitement for the day. I took care of everything and cleared both our schedules."

Beauty leaned in closer to his warm body. Thank you, was all she could manage as they walked through the doors and out to the car.

They were quiet on the ride home. The evil Troll had found out Beauty and the Princess were staying with Knight at his house, and threw a spoiled brat fit about it. Even going as far as to drive a truck through the locked gates at the end of the drive. In Beauty's opinion, the Troll was as bat-shit crazy as the Beast.

As the silence in the car allowed her to get lost in her ever-growing thoughts of their situation. the only solace she could find was in the strong but gentle grip of Knight's hand over hers. Since they were no longer headed to the haven of Knight's property, they had to go to the apartment. A place where Beauty did not feel safe since the Beast knew its location. She sighed heavily and placed her head against the glass of her window. She was staring wearily at the passing landscape when she glimpsed a car in the side mirror. It was the Beast and he was following them. Alarm set in as she shot up in her seat and gripped Knight's hand.

"He's behind us."

Knight glanced in the rearview mirror then over his shoulder. A muttered curse escaped his lips. With a calm tone, he instructed Beauty.

"Call the police. Tell them the make of his vehicle and ours. Explain the situation."

Beauty pulled out her cell phone with shaking hands. When the dispatcher answered, Beauty did her best to explain, but was so frightened that Knight ended up taking the phone and relaying all the vital information.

Knight kept calm and tried to soothe Beauty. "It's ok, baby. The cops are on their way."

Beauty kept her eyes trained on the mirror, watching as the Beast accelerated. He was coming up behind them so fast, Beauty feared he would run into them or run them off the road."

With a panic-stricken face she turned to Knight. "I love you."

Knight stayed calm and squeezed her now clammy hands. "I love you too, baby. I told you it's going to be ok."

Beauty was a jumble of fear and nerves as the Beast's car grew so close his bumper was almost touching theirs. Knight did not speed up or try to evade the Beast. He stayed within the speed limit and kept watch in the rearview. Beauty was on the verge of screaming when they passed the police cruiser. She turned to peer through the back window and watched as the car swiftly turned with red and blue lights flashing. The cruiser quickly caught up to the Beast and he started to slow down, giving them some breathing room. Beauty could feel the adrenaline coursing through her veins. Knight started slowing down as well.

"What are you doing? Don't stop!" Her voice had taken on a shrill tone with the last few words.

Knight pulled over to the side of the road, not far, just in front of where the officer had the Beast pulled over. Beauty watched in dismay as the officer spoke with the Beast and another police cruiser pulled up behind the other cruiser. The new officer walked pass the Beast's vehicle and toward theirs. Knight rolled down the window and greeted the officer. The officer was pleasant, but stern, with a deep, heavily accented twang.

"You folks doing ok?"

Beauty nodded as Knight answered for them.

"Yes, Sir. We are better now that y'all are here."

He then gave the officer a quick run-down of the situation. The officer was an older man but still in decent shape. He hooked his beefy thumbs on either side of his gun belt and listened. He would occasionally nod or look toward the Beast's vehicle, each movement causing the setting sun to glint off the metal on his uniform. Beauty quietly watched the exchange, a churning of anxiety growing in her empty belly. The first signs of nausea starting. She could feel her skin growing clammier with each passing minute. When Knight was done, the officer looked between him and Beauty, as if taking their measure and concluding something only he knew. After a long pause, he nodded and patted the top of the car.

"Alright then, let me go talk to the other officer. You folks wait here."

Beauty turned and watched the man walk toward the other officer and began talking. She could feel the Beast's glare boring a hole into her soul. Even though he was some distance away, she could make out the scowl on his face. His piercing blue eyes hidden behind dark sunglasses. He was clenching and unclenching his hands on the steering wheel. The movement so fierce she could see his knuckles go white with each flex of his fingers. A gentle touch of Knight's hand to her chin brought Beauty's attention to his handsome face. A reassuring smile played on his lips.

"We are ok, baby. He can't touch you anymore."

Beauty wanted to believe Knight with every piece of her being, but she could not shake the traitorous, niggling sense of doubt gnawing at her insides like a parasite.

As she stared into Knight's unflinching gaze of love, the officer returned and knocked on the roof of the car. This broke the connection between her and Knight. He turned to look at the officer and smiled. The officer nodded, his voice clipped and efficient.

"Looks like you are all good to go. We have instructed him not to try and contact either of you in any way. He has also been told to stay away from both of you."

Knight placed his hand out the window and the officer shook it.

"Thank you, Sir."

With a nod, the officer walked back to his cruiser. Both officers waited until the Beast pulled away and sped past them. Beauty watched as his tail lights disappeared into the distance.

Knight turned to her, a smile on his lips. "See, baby, it's like I said. You are safe now. The hardest part is over."

Beauty felt the fear and anxiety clawing at her already raw nerves. She knew the Beast. This was far from over.

35

No peace for the wicked...

Beauty had been right in her prediction that this fight was not over. No, it was just beginning, and the Beast was going to use every dirty trick in his bag of crazy.

The Beast took none of the officer's warnings to heart. Instead, the very night of all the chaos, he began his stalking. It started with phone calls. Beauty's phone would ring, and the caller ID would show it was her mother calling. When she answered, it would be the Beast. Beauty would hang up and the phone would immediately start ringing again. This time it would show her father was calling. She would

answer, and it would be the Beast. This continued with every family member or contact she
had until she could no longer take it and turned
the phone off.

Next, he started with social media. The
Beast befriended all of Beauty's and Knight's
friends. Then, he wrote a scathing and degrad-
ing message releasing it for all of them to see.
His social media attacks extended to sending
her message after message, covering all spec-
trums of crazy. One message would be begging
that they work it out and he forgave her. The
next message would be full of threats and hate.
The Beast was clearly losing his ever-loving shit
and with each unstable action, Beauty's fear
grew.

Knight stayed by her side twenty-four
seven, but Beauty knew that he would not be
able to do this forever. Knight had obligations
to the military and would have to be gone for a
weekend each month. His weekend was quickly
approaching, and Beauty was worried about
what the Beast might do. The monster had taken
to sitting outside the apartment and her job. He
would turn up anywhere she went. Knight was
always with her, so the Beast never approached
and always parked his car just far enough away

to look like he was just going to a store near wherever Beauty was at.

Beauty contacted the police and tried to get a protective order, but since there had not been an act of violence in the previous thirty days, the courts would not give her one. The authorities told her that if she wanted a restraining order, she would need to retain a lawyer and pay for one, since those were considered a civil matter.

Beauty could not afford a lawyer and she was not going to pass on the problem to Knight. If he spent any money on Beauty that could be traced, the Troll would use it against him in their divorce. It was a hot mess of a situation on all fronts and the Beast was taking full advantage.

Beauty became very guarded and aware of her surroundings always. Even sitting in her office, she felt like she was being watched. When she was home, she felt uneasy and jumpy. Her life had morphed into one where she was always looking over her shoulder. The thought of living like this forever was taxing. The stress and anxiety were starting to affect her physical and mental health. Beauty stopped eating because she could not keep food down. She barely slept and when she was able to fall asleep, it was restless because she was plagued by night-mares.

Knight was a rock for Beauty through the whole ordeal. He was always reassuring her and protecting her. The Princess was under constant guard as well. A male family member was with her always. Beauty knew the Beast would use anyone or anything to get to her, even the Princess.

The torment had been going on for weeks when it finally happened. It was a typical weekday night and Beauty had been exhausted from all the stress and had managed to fall asleep. Knight was in bed next to her, out like a light. He could sleep through a tornado. The man was literally dead to the world once he was out. The Princess was the same way. She had always been a sound sleeper. With everything that was going on, Beauty had Knight move the Princess's bed into their room. She wanted her daughter close.

Beauty was a light sleeper and so it was no surprise if she woke up to a noise, especially with how on edge she was. The room was completely dark when Beauty groggily opened her eyes. Everything in the room was blurs of dark shadows. Had that been a click of a lock and a door creaking? She lay there completely still, mentally clocking every sound. The deep even breathing of Knight. The Princess's soft, little purring snores. Everything seemed ok. Nothing seemed out of place.

After a few moments, she chalked it up to nerves and closed her eyes. That was when a rough hand that smelled of tobacco and motor grease closed over her mouth. Beauty's eyes shot open. The Beast's face was mere inches from her own. The clouds outside must have shifted, letting in eerie shards of moonlight through the blinds. The soft, glowing light illuminated his hard-scowling face and glinted off something metal in his other hand. A gun! Terror rose up inside of Beauty, but she lay completely still. She recognized the all too familiar insanity cloaking the monster before her. A myriad of fears ran through her brain in those seconds she stared into his cold eyes. What did he plan to do? Was he going to kill them all? Please God, don't let him hurt Knight or the baby. They were her whole life and she wanted nothing more than for them to be safe. A single tear slid from each corner of Beauty's eyes. The Beast sneered down and motioned with the hand carrying the gun. He placed the gun barrel over his lips in a shushing motion and slowly removed his hand from Beauty's mouth. Her eyes darted around the room, but she stayed silent. She did not know what to do. If she woke Knight, the Beast would shoot him. So, Beauty did the only thing she could do. She slid quietly from the bed and stood before the Beast. He gripped her upper arm and turned her toward the door. Placing the gun barrel at the small of her back, he silently marched her from the room and across the apartment. The apartment was eerily dark, but he navigated them around the furniture with ease. Beauty realized two things in that moment. He was taking her to the guest bathroom which was the farthest room from the bedroom where Knight and the baby slept. And he knew the layout of the apartment, which meant he had been in it at some point.

He led her inside the bathroom and shut the door behind them. That old familiar numbness began to settle in. Beauty would suffer. She knew this without a doubt, but she would do it if it meant he would get what he came for and leave. Beauty knew the Beast planned to rape her. She had known it the minute he started leading her toward the bathroom. He was an animal with animalistic needs to claim what he believed was his.

He flicked the light on and turned her around to face him. She squinted at the sudden light and tried to shield her face. As her eyes adjusted, she began to really see the Beast. He was thinner, with almost a gaunt appearance, but the rage bubbling just beneath the surface still made him menacing. His clothing hung from his frame like tattered rags. Nothing matched, and he had an unkempt beard on his face. The pupils of his eyes were dilated to tiny points. He was clearly strung out. He looked dirty and smelled as if he had not showered in all the weeks since she had left him. Her stomach lurched at the thought of what he was about to do to her. Part of her brain screamed at her to fight back, but it was overruled by the scared girl who had suffered so much at the hands of this monster.

Beauty eyed his gun for a split second. The Beast smirked and placed it on her temple. His voice was like a thousand tiny razors slicing her skin.

"Lie down on the floor!"

Beauty moved like a zombie as she did what she was told. She turned her head to the side and felt herself detach from the situation. Her mind was starting to shield her from what was to come. She barely registered as he unbuckled his belt, and his pants made a clinking sound as they hit the floor. Next came the rip of her underwear, now mere shreds of lace discarded. He lifted her oversized sleep shirt to bare her intimate parts and breasts. The tile was hard and cold against her bare skin. His body felt heavy and clammy as he lay atop her, spreading her legs wide with his hips. He used one hand to grip her hip. His voice was raspy and his breath foul.

"Put your arms above your head."

With robotic movements, Beauty did as she was told, and he gripped both her wrists with his other powerful hand.

Beauty wanted to cry out, but she was paralyzed in a state of total numbness. She lay there limply as he entered her and invaded the most intimate part of her body. His thrusts were hard and rough, the grip he held on her thigh and wrists so tight it was bruising. He was hurting her in so many ways. Taking from her and breaking her. Silent tears spilled from the corners of her tightly clinched eyes. Everything became singular in those moments. The only sounds she heard were his hot breaths in her ear and one word repeated over and over... MINE.

The only thing she could feel was the pain. She tried to block it out and go to another place, but she stayed too present in those moments and she felt it all. When he finally finished with one brutal thrust and she felt his hot seed flood into her, there was no relief it was over. There was only nothingness. Beauty wanted to curl into a ball and cry until she had no tears left, but she stayed motionless as he got up. She cracked open one eyelid and watched as he redressed and picked up what was left of her lace underwear. He scowled down at her with a look of disgust and pleasure.

"Get up. You made a mess. Clean it up."

Beauty slowly sat up and pulled down her shirt. She looked at the blood mixed with his seed coating her legs and the floor. With those same robotic movements, she stood and grabbed a dirty towel from the hamper. Her arms and legs were shaky as she bent to clean the mess from the once pristine white tile. Within moments, the floor was clean, and it looked as if nothing had happened there. Beauty looked at the Beast, wondering what his next move would be. He took a step toward her and she reflexively stepped back. The small bathroom grew smaller as he advanced.

She eyed the gun tucked into the waist of his jeans. He smirked at her and shook one finger.

"Ah, Ah, Ah, my Beauty. I'm not done with you yet. Be a good girl and I will let that fucker live. I shouldn't since he dared to try and take what is mine, but I am feeling generous."

Beauty watched in horror as the Beast pulled a length of cord from his back pocket.

"Give more those wrists."

Beauty stared blankly as if she had not heard him. Her mind racing as she tried to find an escape. The beast jerked one of her already sore and bruising wrists and started to wrap the cord around it. She was still standing there like a robot, trying to figure out what to do, when he grasped her other wrist and began tying it up as well. Panic started rising and she opened her mouth to scream. But before she got anything out, the Beast had stuffed her lace underwear into her mouth and was securing another cord between her lips. She thrashed for a moment and the Beast gripped her hard, whispering into her ear.

"If you wake up the Knight in Shining Armor, he will die tonight. You wouldn't want our little Princess to see that, would you?"

This statement stilled Beauty, all the fight immediately leaving her body.

"Good girl."

He started walking through the dark apartment. Beauty's mind was reeling with possibilities. Did he plan to kill her? Where was he taking her? Oh God, she would never see the Princess or Knight again. What if they thought she left them? Oh God, what about her poor little girl?

Beauty's last thought was answered as she caught sight of the open front door. A short pudgy silhouette stood with its back to her. It was only an outline at first, but as Beauty was dragged closer, she made out who stood there. It was the vilest woman on the planet. The Drama Queen. Beauty felt bile rise in her throat and did her best to choke it back down. It was then the evil bitch stepped into the dim porch light and Beauty's heart stopped. She almost lost her footing and fell as she caught sight of her worst nightmare. The vile creature was holding something. Not something. Someone. A beautiful little face was sleeping soundly on the evil bitch's shoulder, the rest of her body cradled in beefy arms. A cascade of soft, honey golden curls falling down the Drama Queen's arm and back, and the sweet face of the Princess mostly hidden behind them. That evil bitch had her baby.

The Beast pushed Beauty out the door right as his evil sister looked back. "Got everything you wanted?"

"Yup"

"Me too," was her response as she rubbed circles on the Princess's back.

Beauty began to fight then, hoping anyone would hear. She did not care about anything but getting the Princess away from these monsters.

The Beast growled and moved quickly. Beauty didn't see the gun or his hand, but she felt the impact. Pain shot through her head and a warm sticky substance began to flow into her left eye. The Beast threw her limp body over one shoulder and began to carry her. Beauty felt dizziness and pain assail her as she bounced. Her head was too heavy to lift and felt like it weighed five hundred pounds. She tried to kick and flail her arms, but her limbs would not cooperate. There was a rushing sound in her ears and her vision began to blur. Her last fleeting thought before the darkness took her was, "Not my baby. Please, let this be a nightmare."

36

A Knight's Tale...

Early morning rays of sunlight peeked through the cheap blinds of the apartment window. I had slept like the dead and was too groggy to wake. Out of instinct, I rolled over and reached out to pull my Beauty closer to me. I loved wrapping my strong arms around her tiny frame and hearing her sigh of contentment. I had never felt a love like this. Her and our daughter, yes, our daughter, were my entire world. I did not care about my little Princess's DNA, because that little girl was mine in every way that really mattered. I would die for my girls and protect them with my life.

As I patted the bed where my Beauty should have been, I realized it was empty. I sat up and looked around. The room was silent, and the bedding was turned down on her side. Maybe she was in the kitchen? She had not been sleeping well and was usually up before me. I strained to listen for sounds from the other rooms, but I heard nothing. There was no low hum of a television. No clattering in the kitchen, and no sweet female voices filling this tiny home. Worry filled me as I jumped out of bed and checked to see if the Princess was still sleeping, but I found her bed empty too. In a rush, I ran through the apartment, checking every room. The only thing that was out of place was the guest bathroom light being on. I ran to the front door and found it unlocked. The fear inside me increased as I swung it open and peered outside. Beauty's car was gone. They were gone. Where were my girls?

I stood staring at the spot where her car had been, rubbing my chin as I tried to puzzle out what was going on. A growing sense of something horribly wrong was filling me with panic. I headed back into the bedroom to find my phone. I will call Beauty and she'll assure me they're fine. Maybe they just ran to the store or got breakfast. It was not like her to leave without me, but maybe the baby was hungry. I kept telling myself... they are fine. They're coming back. My mantra repeated over and over only heightened the worry as I tore the room apart searching for my cell phone. I damn near leapt for joy when I found it under the bed. Please don't let the battery be dead. Yes, ten percent and blinking green with a text message. I quickly opened the message app and smiled to see it was from Beauty. Relief flooded me until I opened the message.

Beauty: I don't love you. I never did. We're going to live with the Beast. We're going to be a family. Leave us alone and NEVER contact me again.

My knees gave out as I slumped to the bed. My chest tightened with unshed tears. This couldn't be happening. This couldn't be real. I dialed Beauty's number and it went straight to voicemail. I tried again and got the same results. After the third time, I threw my phone down on the bed and hung my head. Cradling it with my hands, I felt a pain so deep my soul began to fracture. My girls were gone. Two pieces of my heart were gone. How am I supposed to live without those missing pieces?

37

HELL…

I t wasn't a nightmare. Beauty woke up from her unconsciousness and found herself in a small dark space. It felt like her body was racing along while she lay still inside this carpet-lined space. She looked around in the darkness and as her eyes adjusted, she registered her surroundings. She was in the trunk of a car. She used her bound hands to feel around for anything. She felt rigid plastic beneath her fingertips. Triangular shaped plastic filled with paper. Binders? Several binders. She felt like she had been gutted when realization hit. She was in her trunk. The trunk of her car.

Those monsters had taken her car and made it look like she left of her own free will. Beauty thrashed and screamed through the gag, but it was useless. Her head ached, hell, her whole body ached. Her heart hurt the worst. Fear and worry for the Princess was at the forefront of her mind. God, she wanted Knight. She wanted him to swoop in and whisk them away from these vile monsters. Make all the bad disappear.

Beauty had no sense of time, so she was not sure how long she stayed in that trunk. When she felt the vehicle slowing and pulling up an incline, she knew they must have arrived at their intended destination.

She readied herself. This time she would fight. For herself and her daughter. She heard muffled voices as she waited. Only the Beast's and the Drama Queen's, nothing of the Princess. Beauty's heart raced as she heard the trunk unlatch. It was still dark outside and only the overhead light of the trunk illuminated the Beast's face. He was turned away, talking to his retched sister. Beauty seized that moment and kicked out as hard as she could. Her foot connected with his jaw and she felt the crack of bone. A sense of pride shot through her. The Beast reeled back as she tried to scramble from the trunk. It was hard to do with her hands bound. She managed to tumble onto the cement and got up on her feet, when she felt fingers digging into the back of her head and grabbing her hair. The Beast jerked her backwards with a curse and she landed hard on the cement.

"YOU BITCH!" he yelled as he spat blood beside her on the ground.

Beauty stared up at him with murder in her eyes, but the Beast only laughed cruelly and jerked her up by the hair. He brought his face close to hers and she could smell the metallic scent of blood.

"Oh, look at you. Finally got some fight in you. I love it when you fight. Makes the winning so much more fun."

Beauty would have spat in his face and clawed out his eyes if she hadn't been bound and gagged.

With a shove, he pushed her away from the car and toward a house she knew all too well. It was the Drama Queen's home. Beauty shuddered at the sight of it. The lair of a monster just as sexually perverted and sadistic as the Beast.

He led her through the house and into a bedroom near the back. When Beauty entered the dark room, she could only make out large shapes. Once the Beast turned on the light, she did a double take and stopped moving. Her brain barely able to register what was in front of her. Fear rose inside her chest. There was a wrought iron bed with no bedding. Its only adornments a plastic covering and strong metal shackles secured to the foot and headboards. The one window in the room looked as if it had been soundproofed with foam and blankets. A dresser was set against one wall, with all kinds of toys and torture devices littering the top.

Beauty stayed motionless as the Beast began to move around her.

"If you hit me again, I will take it out on the Princess. Do you understand?"

Beauty's eyes blazed with fire, but she nodded.

He proceeded to untie her hands and strip her naked. Then, he roughly bound her feet to the bed. She shook as he raised each arm and secured her sore wrists. Then, he stood over her, gazing down at his prisoner with what Beauty could only describe as pleasure. She tried to talk, and the Beast placed a hand on her head to untie the gag.

He stopped. "If you cry out, you will never see the Princess again. Do you understand me?"

Beauty nodded her head in agreement.

He removed the gag and she worked her jaw, trying to get the dry fabric taste from her mouth. Her lips were dry, and her jaw ached. Her voice was raspy from the soreness in her throat.

"Where is my daughter?"

"In safe hands."

Beauty glared at him. "You can't do this. This is illegal. It's kidnapping."

Anger spiked through the Beast. "I can do whatever the fuck I want to you and HER! You belong to me. I cannot kidnap what is already mine. You will understand that fact and accept it before you ever leave this room or see the baby. I will break you and remold you and we will be a family again."

Beauty felt tears well up as her voice cracked with the pain. "Please, don't do this. Please."

The Beast just sneered down at her. "Oh, I love it when you beg. It makes breaking you so much more fun."

The Beast moved away from her then and started undressing. She began to cry harder. Her insides still ached from his last brutal attack. He stood before her naked and ready to do more damage and she clenched her eyes shut. But when she didn't feel the bed dip with his weight, she slightly opened one eye. She spotted him with his back turned to her. He was standing in front of the dresser, choosing what kind of torture he would inflict on her. When he turned, he had a few large toys and a paddle tipped with spikes.

Beauty whimpered with fear as he approached her. In silence, he laid down all his toys on the bed. When the pain started, Beauty checked out. Occasionally, she would register a sound not being made by him. Once, she looked up and caught the Drama Queen watching, her face a mixture of fascination and pleasure. Beauty learned several things that night. Her body had a high tolerance for pain before passing out. The Beast and his sister were far more sadistic than she could have ever imagined, and the Beast had acquired a few more fetishes that she had known nothing about. The most horrifying was his new fascination with strangulation and revival. Beauty didn't know true madness until the mad monster repeatedly strangled her until she lost consciousness, only to revive her so he could do it again. She was violated in so many ways, most people would have lost their minds.

When the Beast was done, he dropped down beside her bloody, bruised, and cigarette burned body. She was unable to move. Her body and mind in physical, emotional, and mental agony. The Beast was determined to break her completely this time and Beauty didn't know if she would survive it. The only thoughts that kept her sane were of Knight and the Princess. She hated to mix the two separate worlds of her life and wanted none of the Beast's bad to taint the good, but Beauty was desperate. She was afraid she might be dying. The pain was so bad she needed an escape and the only place she could turn to was her imagination.

So, as the monster lay snoring beside her, she closed her tired eyes that were raw from crying and tried to see the faces of her loved ones. She imagined the Princess and Knight playing at the park. She tried to grasp onto the sounds of their laughter, over the thudding of her heart. She pictured her daughter's sweet smile and beautiful eyes. She imagined the Knight wrapping his strong arms around her and keeping her safe. The last image caused more tears to flow. She wondered what he was doing. What he was thinking? Would he look for them? God, she hoped he would try to get them back. She prayed for help of any kind until she could not pray anymore, and the exhaustion took her.

38

There is no fairy-tale life...

I f Beauty still believed in fairy-tales, this would be the part where Knight would ride in on his white horse and rescue them and they would live happily ever after. But there was no such thing as a fairy-tale. Not for Beauty. None of her prayers were answered. None of her silent pleas for help were heard. None of her dreams of a rescue came to pass. The torture continued and morphed into more acts of vile degradation than Beauty could have ever believed possible.

In those first days, the Beast cut her off from all communication. He sent texts to all her loved ones stating she was not coming back and wanted to be with the Beast. When Knight refused to accept this, Beauty was forced to read a script the Beast had written in a particularly heartbreaking phone conversation. He made her tell Knight she wanted nothing to do with him. That she had never loved him and wanted the Beast. His voice had gutted her, devoid of all emotion.

"As you wish."

Beauty had been unable to shed the tears she wanted to desperately spill at that moment. She could physically feel her heart shattering into a million pieces and it was worse than any pain the Beast had ever inflicted on her.

Her family had reacted with shame and disgust. As they had always done every time they thought Beauty had chosen to go back to the Beast willingly. Her mother had responded to the texts from the Beast with a simple. "You are stupid." Her father and brother disowned her again. Beauty had no one, not even the Princess, because she had no idea where her precious daughter was. She only saw her two vile captors and they delighted in all agony they could inflict on her, including keeping the whereabouts of her child secret.

The Beast had taken leave from his job and devoted every moment to breaking Beauty. She never knew which Beast she would encounter. All his faces hurt her in some way. He teetered on the edge of insanity. One minute being a violent Beast, the next, lying beside her like a hurt child and caressing her bare skin, whispering how much he loved her and that he could not lose her. She was his and always would be.

The new degradations included never being unchained to use the restroom. She was forced to defecate on herself, then be punished for making a mess. She was given sponge baths sporadically and rarely fed. The Drama Queen and the Beast only gave her just enough sustenance to survive.

The Beast would brutally rape her using objects to penetrate her insides until she bled. The blood made him frenzied and more aroused, so he would enter after ripping her insides. Beauty could feel something was very wrong inside her. The pain from each attack was growing worse. She was never allowed to heal and was hurting constantly. The Beast had also taken to photographing and videoing the vile attacks, so he could watch them later and prepare for the next round of abuse. When he first started making the videos, he told Beauty he had decided to make money off her by posting them to pornographic websites online. He also posted naked photos of her for all the world to see. He wanted to take any dignity she had left. Beauty was no longer called by her name. He only referred to her as his "whore."

There were times in the first few weeks where Beauty was unchained, cleaned, and dressed. The first time, she felt a spark of hope that the Beast had grown tired of her and she was going to be released. But she quickly found this was not the case. It was all another part of the Beast's plan. Beauty was brought outside into a fenced-in yard. The sunlight blinded her. She was instructed to sit on a bench and smile. The Beast sat beside her and placed his arm around her. His voice a low, menacing whisper.

"You better look fucking happy and in love... or else."

Beauty knew what the "or else" was and did her best, but she knew her eyes would be devoid of all emotion and give her away. The Drama Queen took several shots where Beauty was posed like a doll in various, fake, happy positions. The Beast even forced her to kiss him. Once the photo shoot was done, she was taken back to her prison, undressed and rechained. This happened about twice a week for several weeks. After the first photo shoot, Beauty found out why. The Beast was posting the photos on various social media accounts including her own, to make everyone believe she was indeed exactly where she wanted to be. He delighted in texting or emailing the photos to Knight and her family, then carrying on conversations as if he were Beauty. She would watch with disgust as he sat beside her on the bed, grinning and reading off the hurtful things he would say and the responses. He was solidifying the lie and pushing everyone further and further away, until they all believed it so thoroughly that they thought she was just as sick and twisted as he was.

As the hours turned into days, Beauty lost count of how long she had been held captive. She grew thinner and sicker. Something inside her soul was breaking. The emotional and mental pain taking as much of a toil on her as the physical. She tried to hold on to those memories of the Princess, and Knight's beautiful face, but as she was reduced to nothing, even their images began to dim until she could no longer see anything but the darkness of her mind.

She called out for her mother and father, but the Beast would laugh and tell her no one was coming for her. She had no one and believed she was near death. At some point, she had lost her will to live and just became a catatonic shell of a person. When the Beast realized he had broken her spirit, he began to slowly allow her more freedom.

He started by unchaining her and allowing her to use the restroom while he watched. She was never left alone but she could bathe herself and wear clothing. She was given more food and regained some strength. The Beast even stopped brutally attacking her, opting to "make love" to her. The lack of torture allowed her to start healing, but the persistent pain inside her never went away. She did not know for sure how long she had been in this state, but she could tell it was getting close to the start of the school year, and she wondered if that was why things were changing. The Princess had to attend school.

One day, the Beast came in and declared that he had found them a house and they would be moving. He told her this as he unshackled her and put pants on her. It felt strange to Beauty to have her legs covered again. Up to that point, the most she had been allowed to wear was a large t-shirt. When he placed a pair of shoes in front of her, she was afraid to move. Was this another of his tricks? The Beast looked at her like she was the village idiot.

"Put your shoes on. We're leaving. I told you we are moving."

With frail arms and robotic movements, Beauty did as she was told and then waited for further instruction. The Beast sneered at her.

"That's my good little whore! Now, look happy. I brought you a present."

Beauty stiffened and wanted to recoil. Normally, his presents were full of pain, but a sound of tiny tinkling laughter from outside the door caught Beauty's attention and she clumsily stood and tried to move toward the door. Her progress was slow-going as she was still very weak and in constant pain. The Beast opened the door and braced Beauty with a hand around her waist. He propelled her forward, toward the sound of the laughter. With each step closer, Beauty felt her heart thud and a small spark of hope grew. When she finally caught sight of her gorgeous little Princess playing, she cried out with a cracked and raspy voice.

"Baby!"

The Princess immediately turned and ran toward Beauty, a huge smile on her face.

"Mama! Mama! I have missed you so much!"

Beauty tried to bend down to capture her little angel, but she was so weak. When the little girl ran into her with the full force of her tight hug, Beauty collapsed to the ground, falling on her back and wrapping the little girl in her weak arms. The two tumbled and the Princess giggled as she landed on top of Beauty. She rose up to meet her eyes.

"Are you feeling better, Mommy? Daddy said you were sick and that's why I couldn't see you. He said that's why I had to spend time with my other Grandmas and Grandpas."

Beauty just stared at the little girl as tears streamed down her face. The Princess gave her a worried look.

"Did I hurt you, Mommy? Are you ok? Daddy said you were better. I wouldn't have hugged you so hard if you were still sick."

Beauty cradled the little girl's head to her nose and breathed in the scent of her child. With a hoarse whisper, she told her angel, "I'm ok, baby. Mommy is ok. I just really missed you."

The little girl giggled.

"I missed you too, Mommy, but I'm here now, and Daddy says we have a new house and I can go to a new school and make new friends. He said he set us all up while you were sick."

Beauty held on to her little girl for dear life.

"Ok, baby. I love you so much. Mommy loves you so much. I missed you every second of every day. Thinking of you was the only thing that got Mommy through." Beauty stopped for a moment and forced out the next words. "Thinking of you was the only thing that got me through my sickness."

It was then the Beast chose to break up their reunion.

"Alright, alright, we need to go. You two can talk in the car."

The Beast pulled Beauty to her feet, but she never let go of the Princess's hand as they were escorted outside into the blinding sunlight. Beauty only looked back once and saw the vile Drama Queen smirking a knowing smile. Beauty wished she would never see that grotesque creature again.

Beauty sat in the back and still held the Princess's hand as the little girl told her all about the fun things she had done over the summer. She told Beauty of all the relatives she had met and stayed with. All the places she visited. No wonder Beauty had never heard the child in the Drama Queen's home. They had arranged to have her child carted from one family to another for two months. Some of which lived far away. Beauty shuddered at the thought of her daughter spending time with all the different members of the Beast's family. She also realized that she had been their captive for two months. It had felt like forever. She eyed the back of the Beast warily as she listened to the Princess. She wondered what was next in this twisted, sadistic version of life. When they had to stop for gas and the Beast went to pay, the Princess tugged on her shirt.

"Mommy, I was not allowed to talk to my Grandma, the Queen. Daddy got very mad when I asked about Knight. He said I was never to mention him ever again. He said if I did, he would spank me. Is Knight ok?"

Beauty could feel the sadness and her voice cracked a little. "I'm sorry, baby. I'm sorry you haven't gotten to speak to Grandma. I haven't spoken to her either. And Knight, well, that subject upsets Daddy so let's not mention it around him. But when he's gone, you can talk to me. Ok?"

The Princess looked up at her with big, sad eyes.

"I miss him, Mommy. I think about him every day. Do you think he misses me?"

Beauty wrapped her arms around the Princess and whispered into her hair.

"Oh baby, I know he misses you every day. I miss him too, baby. I miss him more than Mommy could put into words. But we cannot talk about him if Daddy is around. He will get very mad. Ok? Do you understand?"

The little girl pulled back from Beauty and looked at her with eyes far too knowing for a child of her age.

"I understand, Mommy. I promise." Then, the little angel made a zipping motion across her lips with her fingers and Beauty had to laugh at how adorable she was.

This little girl was the only joy she had in life. The thought halted her laughter and made her still, with her arms around her daughter. Her thoughts froze her in fear. What if the Beast tried to take her again? Beauty inwardly cursed. She would die this time before that happened again. Just then, the Beast got back into the car.

"My girls ready to see their new home?"

The Princess smiled and clapped. "Yay!!!!"

Beauty met the Beast's eyes in the rearview mirror and she pasted on a fake smile as she nodded in agreement to the Princess's joyful response.

The Beast smiled back, and Beauty thought she caught a glint of victory in his cold blue eyes.

39

A New House of Horrors

T he Beast pulled up to a tiny, shit brown, brick old house only about a block from his work. The proximity to his job was not lost on Beauty. She knew it was so he could keep a close eye on the house and her. When she stepped inside, she immediately noticed the darkness. There were black-out curtains on every window and sparse furniture. A tiny kitchen with old linoleum and wood paneled walls. The carpet was dingy and outdated. A futon in place of a couch. The hallway was long and dark with three doors. The first was a room decorated for the Princess. A tiny bed, TV, and few toys. The Beast had obviously done the decorating. Across from her room was an outdated bathroom. At the end of the hall was the darkest room. A mattress was laid out on the floor with the black-out curtains giving it the look of a dungeon or torture chamber. Beauty hated every inch of her new prison without visible bars. The security system and cameras seemed to have been the Beast's most expensive purchases and additions to the old house. This fact was not lost on Beauty. When he was away he would be able to watch her... always.

On the journey to the new prison, he had made it a point to tell her that he had activated a security system on her vehicle. It enabled him to see where it was at all times. How far it had traveled and even shut it off remotely if he needed to. The Beast had covered everything. She would be a prisoner in this house and everything she did would be monitored. He even found delight in letting her know his vile sister could watch anytime she wanted. That revelation had made Beauty want to vomit. She was nothing more than a pawn to the sadistic pair. With all her contact to the outside world cut off, Beauty was alone with the Beast and his sadistic proclivities. She had been abandoned by Knight and her family. It hurt her to know they thought so little of her, and knew nothing of her true self, that they would give up on her so easily.

Beauty's days became a routine of pain and loneliness. The Beast worked a night shift which meant he slept during the day. After Beauty got the Princess ready for school, he would drive her to school himself since Beauty was not allowed to drive anywhere. He would occasionally let Beauty ride with them, but she was never allowed to go anywhere on her own. In the mornings, he would torture her with whatever his desire was that day. Then, he would sleep. Beauty was expected to stay in bed with him and not move. He would hold her tightly and if she tried to move, he would wake and ask.

"Where do you think you're going?"

She only left to go to the restroom and always returned immediately. If she took too long and he had to come looking for her, she would pay the price in blood and pain.

In the afternoons, she would wake him in time to pick up the Princess and then prepare dinner. During this time, she was expected to pretend they were a normal happy family. She was expected to mask the pain and the bruises.

The Beast had a very short temper. More so than before. His patience with the Princess was non-existent. He was treating her as if she had cheated on him as well. Being very passive-aggressive and ignoring her when she tried to speak to him. When he tried to punish the Princess, the punishments were very harsh. Beauty would get between the Beast and her daughter, placing the child in her room, and taking whatever beating he had planned for the little girl.

Beauty knew her daughter could hear him hurting her. Calling her a whore and punishing her. But she tried to shield her daughter as much as possible. It broke Beauty more and more as she watched the light die in her child's eyes. The Princess was becoming like Beauty, living a life of fear. After months of this, Beauty worked up the courage to try and escape while the Beast was sleeping. It was early, around dawn on a weekend, and she quietly stole the keys and took the Princess out to the car. They were in the car and she had just started it up when her window was broken by the Beast's fist. Beauty looked into his terrifying face and told the Princess to run. At first, the little girl had been too scared to leave her mother, but as the Beast flung open the driver's side door and started punching Beauty, the little girl took off. Beauty fought back as the Beast tried to strangle her with the seat belt and continued to punch her with his iron fists. She somehow managed to break free of the seat belt and crawled toward the open passenger door. The Beast grabbed hold of one of her legs, but she kicked out as hard as she could with the other and managed to catch him in his balls. As he shrank back in pain, she stumbled from the car and stopped short when she saw the Princess standing there with tears running down her beautiful face. The little girl had witnessed the violence. Beauty rushed toward her daughter at a dead run, swooping her up into her arms and never stopping. She was running as fast as she could down a deserted street when she heard the revving of the engine behind her. She did not need to look over her shoulder. She knew the Beast was after them. She was trying to make it to the park at the end of the street before he caught up to them. She had to leap and roll on the grass, as the front bumper of his car narrowly missed her. He was trying to run her down while she was carrying their daughter. If he had hit them, it would have killed them. Beauty prayed someone would be awake and call the police. Beauty was trying to get up with her daughter still cradled in her arms, when she felt the Beast's finger grab hold of the hair on the back of her head. She let out a cry of pain and clutched the Princess tighter. The little girl was still crying, and Beauty wished she could stop her from experiencing this trauma.

As the Beast dragged Beauty back to his vehicle, he screamed at the Princess to shut up. The little girl did her best to reduce her sobs to sniffles. The Beast put them both into his car and drove them home. Beauty saw no one on the street. It was still eerily quiet, and she knew that there would be no help for her or the Princess that day.

When they covered the short distance and arrived back at the prison, the Beast pointed at the house. No words needed to be said. Beauty exited the car and carried the Princess to her room. She placed the little girl on her bed and kissed her forehead. The Princess looked frightened, with tear-stained cheeks and red-rimmed eyes. Beauty caressed her face in a soothing manner and got the little girl's favorite stuffed animal. She turned the TV on and turned the volume up. Before she left the room, she heard a tiny voice that broke her heart.

"Mommy, I'm scared."

Beauty turned and walked over to her daughter.

"It's ok, baby. Mommy is not going to let him hurt you."

The little girl started shaking her head.

"No, Mommy, I'm scared for you."

Beauty patted her daughter's little belly and gave the best smile she could.

"Don't worry about me, baby. Mommy is tough, and I will be ok. Promise me, no matter what, you will not leave this room."

The Princess gave Beauty a weary look, and Beauty gave her a light kiss on the nose.

"Promise me, baby."

The Princess's voice was a whisper as she clutched her stuffed animal.

"I promise, Mommy."

Beauty left the room and allowed the tears she'd been holding back to fall. The Beast was waiting for her outside the door and merely pointed toward the other bedroom. Beauty obeyed and walked into the room. The Beast shut and locked the door with a quiet click. Then, the real torture began. Beauty never cried out for fear of the Princess hearing. She stayed silent as he beat and raped her violently. Her silence was the only thing she had control of any-more and so she suffered in that silence, praying her daughter could not hear.

40

Can I get a witness?

The only good thing to come out of Beauty's escape attempt was that the Beast started allowing the Queen to see the Princess. This was purely out of selfish reasons on his part. He wanted more time to torture her and realized he could not do that and keep up the façade of a perfect little family, if the Princess kept witnessing his violence. So, after the little girl was sworn to secrecy and threatened if she told, she was allowed to start spending nights and weekends with the Queen.

Beauty was happy her daughter was away from the Beast, but it hurt to be away from her child. Again, she suffered in silence and hid this pain to play the dutiful prisoner of the Beast. When Beauty did see the Princess, she seemed happier and less nervous. With time, Beauty thought she even saw some of the light come back into the girl's eyes.

The Beast had not been able to plan for one thing and that was how much Beauty's body could take. After the constant brutality, he was forced to let her be seen by a doctor. Forced because after one particularly brutal attack, Beauty passed out from the blood loss and pain. Unable to revive her and fearing he might be charged with murder, he quickly dressed himself and Beauty. He moved her to the driveway and called 911. He told the EMs that Beauty had doubled over in pain and collapsed. She was rushed to the hospital and diagnosed with severe endometriosis, multiple ruptured cysts, and internal bleeding. The endometriosis was severe scarring of her uterus and other female parts. The Beast told the doctors that Beauty must have developed the scarring from all her cancer surgeries. When Beauty came to, the Beast was right there in her face, looming over her and gripping her hand so tightly that she knew not to say a word to anyone. Beauty's brain was very foggy from all the drugs they had her on, so it took her a moment to recognize what the doctors were trying to tell her.

"With the severity of the endometriosis, internal bleeding, and history of cancer, it is our recommendation that you have a total hysterectomy."

Beauty blinked at the doctors and tried to process what they were telling her.

"But, but I'm so young. I won't be able to have any more children."

Not that she wanted any more children with the Beast, but she didn't want that option taken away from her.

One of the doctors placed a hand on her leg and gave her a sympathetic look.

"With the amount of damage, children are no longer possible for you."

Beauty felt the tears as she heard the Beast use his fake charming voice. He was putting on a show for the doctors.

"Shhh, baby girl, don't cry. I have you and our daughter. We don't need any more children. Everything will be ok. We have each other and that's all that matters."

Beauty turned her face away from him as he and the doctors conversed. They were making decisions for her. They would be doing the surgery shortly and there was nothing she could do about it. The female doctor came over to her and Beauty recognized her. She knew the Queen. The doctor leaned down and whispered to Beauty.

"Do you want me to call your mother?"

Beauty gave a slight nod, hoping the Beast had not heard. She could feel him staring at her and the female doctor. Beauty let a moan of pain escape and the female doctor stood up.

"She needs more pain meds."

A nurse rushed in then and stuck a surgeon into Beauty's IV. As she watched the liquid snake up the clear tube and enter her hand, the world around Beauty grew fuzzy and she felt like she was floating. She drifted in and out of consciousness until they came to take her to surgery. She thought she saw her mother's worried face as she briefly opened her eyes. The next thing she remembered was someone counting backwards and then darkness.

When Beauty awoke, the pain was intense and everywhere. She felt changed and different. She blinked her groggy eyes open and saw the Beast looking agitated at her side. When she scanned the room and caught sight of her mother, she almost cried. Her mother looked tired and irritated herself. Beauty knew the irritation was probably because of the Beast's presence. She hoped it wasn't because of her. Beauty's throat was so dry, and she was barely able to croak out a request for water.

The Beast was there with a cup and straw. She winced as she sat up in the bed and the Beast handed her three pills to take.

Beauty had grown so accustomed to not questioning his actions that it wasn't until her mother's, voice boomed through the room and startled her that she looked at the pills. They were the same ones the Beast would give her after severe brutality.

"What the HELL do you think you are doing?"

The Queen's eyes were locked on the Beast and Beauty was frozen, unsure if she had done something wrong.

"She's still on IV pain medication and you're trying to give her three pain pills that you got from god knows where. Are you trying to kill her?"

Beauty realized than that the Queen was talking to the Beast. She had already jumped from her seat and moved to take the pills from

Beauty's hand. Beauty looked up at her fierce mother with awe.

"My daughter is coming home with me to recover. I am sure you will insist to be right by her side, but I promise you that she is not leaving here without me."

Beauty watched in stunned silence as the Beast and the Queen stared at each other. Pride swelled in her chest as the Beast was forced to back down. Beauty felt her mother take her hand and give it a reassuring squeeze. Too frightened to look at the Beast, she stared at her mother and watched as her eyes softened. She had disappointed this woman so much, yet she was still there to stand up for Beauty.

Uncharacteristically, the Beast relented with a grumble.

"Fine, we will go to your house."

Beauty could not believe the Beast was allowing this to happen, but she silently thanked God. She had a long recovery in front of her and with her family there, she would hopefully survive it.

Beauty was released from the hospital and told she had at least eight weeks of recovery in front of her. When she stepped into the old house of horrors, she did not feel the same dread she had before. Probably because the new house of horrors had surpassed and replaced what had been done to her in this home. Her mother, father, and brother were all attentive to her and she felt a love she had not felt in a very long time. She had grown so numb and blocked out so much that she no longer knew how to react to kindness. She could tell her mother was suspicious and wanted to ask questions, but the Beast was always around. Beauty could tell that he was coming unraveled at his loss of complete control over her. Having to keep himself in check and continuing the façade of normality was eating away at him with each passing day.

It only took twenty days for him to crack. Beauty was still weak and recovering slowly. It had been just over a year since she and the Princess had been taken from Knight, but she still thought of him daily. It was also her father's birthday and a small celebration was planned. It was late afternoon and Beauty was resting before the celebration. She was suddenly awakened by an agonizing pain in her left side. She knew the feeling, it was one she was all too familiar with. Her ribs had been broken. The Beast had kicked her in the side while she was sleeping. She cried out in pain as he loomed over her.

There was that old rage in his eyes. With labored breaths, Beauty managed to roll from the bed and fall to the floor. The Beast was on her and jerking her up by the hair before she could get her feet. Another cry escaped her lips. The Beast leaned in close enough for her to smell the alcohol on his breath. This explained his total loss of control. His voice was a low menacing whisper.

"Shut your whore mouth, bitch."

Beauty whimpered with pain from her injuries and the Beast threw her across the room as if she were a rag doll. Beauty lay panting on the floor as she heard him approaching. His steel-toed boots were all she saw before he had her jerked up again as he slammed her into a dresser so hard the wall shook. His hands wrapped around her throat as he leaned in close enough that his lips were almost at her ear.

"I planned this from the day I got you back. I took everything from you. Everything! I never wanted you. I never loved you. I can't even stand you. You aren't beautiful to me. You are pathetic, ugly, and fat. I hate your body especially those tiny titties. But I won, you stupid bitch. I won because I took you and I made sure that when I was done with you, you would never be able to bear another man's child. No man will want a bitch who can't have his babies. That is going to be my parting gift, if you survive. Maybe this time, I will just leave you for dead."

Beauty could feel the darkness around her vision as she struggled for breath. Then, there was a loud bang and the Beast's hands were gone from around her throat. She dropped to the ground like a stone, gasping for breath. Her ears were ringing and her vision blurry, but through narrow eyes, she saw her father and brother enraged and beating the Beast. Beauty had to blink several times because she could barely believe her eyes.

Suddenly, her mother rushed in and helped her to her feet. Beauty was slumped against her as they headed toward the door. As Beauty passed the fight, she managed to croak out a few words.

"Don't kill him. He's not worth going to jail over."

Her brother and father both stopped in mid-swing and looked at her. Understanding passing over their faces. She did not want the Beast to ruin their lives as well. Beauty never looked back at the bloody mess on the floor.

Her mother helped her to the car where the Princess was already in her seat. Once the Queen had her secure and was in the driver's seat, she took off quickly and drove them away. After a few miles, she pulled off down a dirt road and looked at Beauty with expectation.

"Where do you want to go? Do you need a hospital? Who do you want me to call?"

Without a single moment of hesitation, Beauty said one word.

"Knight."

The Queen nodded, pulled out her phone and Beauty could hear it ringing. When his familiar voice said, "Hello," her stomach did the flip flop butterfly thing. The Queen handed her the phone.

Beauty's greeting came out quiet and hesitant.

"Hello..."

She heard a long sigh on the other end.

"Beauty."

Tears began to well in her eyes as she tried to speak through them.

"Yes, it's me. I need you. Can we come to your house?"

His voice was immediately alert

"Yes, always. I'm on my way. Do you need

my new address?"

Beauty swallowed. New address? I guess the Troll got his place. A pang of guilt raced through her."

"Yes, please."

She handed the phone to the Queen and leaned her head against the glass as he told her mother the address.

Within seconds, they were on the road again.

41

Home is where the heart is...

It was dark when they arrived. Beauty opened her eyes as the car came to a stop in front of a beautiful, old, two-story residential home. It had white sidings with yellow trimmings, and a charming, white picket fence encompassed the large corner property.

Beauty blinked rapidly, astonishment filling her. She knew this property. It was the lovely home on the corner she had always admired on the few occasions the Beast let her out of the house. It was located only three houses down from the prison she had been confined to for the last year. She had always wondered what it would be like inside the home and harbored an unknown fascination with it. She had even daydreamed a time or two about living a different life in that house. This couldn't be Knights house. Could it?

Her inner monologue was answered as she saw the tall, handsome figure coming down the steps toward the vehicle. Her breath caught at the sight of his lean, muscular body and easy strides. As she caught sight of his handsome face in the dim stream of porch light, something hot and wet started to stream down her face. She was crying. She was really at Knight's home. The man she had been longing for and dreaming of for so long had been only three houses down from her. She cradled her face in her hands and let the realization of all she had been through hit her with a force so strong, silent sobs racked her entire body. She heard the back door open and through blurry eyes, watched as Knight carried a sleeping Princess into his home.

Her mother sat quietly beside her and rubbed her back as she broke down. Beauty looked up to see her mother crying silently as well. The fierce strong woman was crying and that broke her even more. So many of her loved one's lives had been ruined by that monster.

The door beside her opened and drew her attention to the man standing there. She was too ashamed to look at him. Too afraid that he would see what she had become. Too afraid he could see all the vile things that had been done to her. She felt a pair of strong arms wrap around her. The strong arms she had longed for and dreamt of so many times in the past year. She still couldn't believe it was her Knight.

Without effort, he lifted her from the seat and cradled her next to his body. With a strong silence she needed, he carried her inside to a darkened room and sat down on the leather couch. She could feel the cool material beneath her bare feet. Knight still had her clutched tightly in his arms. The embrace felt like he was telling her without words, "I got you and I am never letting you go."

She buried her head in his neck, still crying, and breathed in his clean scent between sobs. He still smelled the same. Like everything good in the world. He smelled like love, and home. Beauty was not sure how long they sat there like that, her cradled in his arms like a small lost child, but he was silent and let her take all the time she needed to break down.

At some point, the Queen had stroked her hair and kissed her goodbye and they were alone in the darkness once again. When she had no more tears left to cry, she lifted her eyes to meet his. Even in the darkness, she could see the emotions swirling within them. He had been so stoic and quiet the entire time. She searched his face and cleared her dry throat as she averted her eyes. The shame of her tainted body and soul too much to bear, while looking at such an honorable man.

"I need you to know that I never wanted to leave you. That was not my choice. I have thought of you and missed you every day since we've been apart. I understand if you have moved on, but I need you to know that for me... the love was real. I will always feel lucky to have been loved by you. Thank you for letting us come here to stay. I will find a way to repay your kindness."

Beauty fidgeted with her fingers in her lap. She sat astride him, looking down and waiting for a response. One of his strong arms was draped behind her, holding her around the waist. Her broken ribs ached but he was careful not to touch her injured side. His other arm was across her bent bare legs. He was silent for a long time, but she could feel him staring at her profile. It felt like the heat of his gaze was boring a hole into the very core of her. His silence was killing her as more shame washed over her with each contemplation of what he could be thinking.

Beauty was trying to work up the courage to move, when she felt the warmth of his hand on her cheek.

He gently turned her face to his and whispered, "Love."

Beauty furrowed her eyes, a look of confusion crossing her face as he continued.

"You said loved. As in past-tense. Not love as in present. It has always been love. I have missed you and that little girl every day and I have loved you every day and I will love you both every day until I die. I will probably love you even after I am gone. Our love isn't something you move on from. Ours is epic and I love you more today than I did yesterday. Tomorrow, I will love you more. I'm not going anywhere, Beauty, and I never will. I am here; however you need me to be. Friend, protector, and your love. For you and the Princess. I promise you that this time... no one will take you from me."

Beauty buried her head in his neck as the tears started again. She thought just when she had no more tears left, he had to go and make that kind of heart-wrenching declaration of love speech.

As she cried tears of joy, this time clutched in the arms of a good man who still loved her, Beauty knew that this time would be different.

As they sat there in the darkness, she felt a feeling she hadn't felt in a very long time.

Hope…

42

Divorcing a Monster, Custody, and Stalking 101...

I t was not all smooth sailing for Beauty and Knight. She had to heal physically, emotionally, and mentally. He had to adjust to a new life with his girls returned. Beauty found out the redheaded witch had been trying every trick in the book to take Knight for her own, but thankfully, his love and resolve had stayed strong. Beauty had never liked that she-devil. But in the end, true love prevailed, and the redheaded witch flew away on her raggedy broom, never to be heard from again. Beauty said good riddance to that!

The Beast was another matter entirely. After her father and brother "detained" the Beast while Beauty and the Princess escaped, he went to live with his vile sister. *Detained* had been the word used on police statements. The officer had pointed out with a grin that her father and brother had actually "beaten the tar out of that boy." But because he obviously had it coming and was on their property, no charges would be filed.

Regrettably, the Beast did not have any charges filed against him either. With the support of Knight, Beauty attempted to get a protective order against the Beast. She was able to get a temporary one, but after six weeks, when it came time for court, the Beast showed up with a copy of every vile photo he had taken of Beauty and served her with divorce papers. Ashamed and not wanting anyone to see the photos, Beauty agreed to drop the protective order in exchange for a mutual restraining order. The Beast would stay away from Beauty and the Princess. She would stay away from him. Beauty thought this would be easy and he would uphold the court order since the Beast had also showed up to court with Drucilla, his young, unfortunate new victim/girlfriend, who was already pregnant with his baby. Also, in attendance was his vile sister. The two women looked like the best of friends and Beauty just shook her head thinking, "Good luck, girl, your life is about to turn to shit."

The Beast stared at Beauty all through the court proceedings and the one time she did meet his gaze, he smirked at her.

As she got up to leave, the district attorney caught her arm and pulled her in close.

"I am going to give you a piece of advice because I saw the way he was looking at you and I read the synopsis of what you suffered at his hands. I will never forget it. So, girlfriend or not, you need to always put your safety at the forefront of your mind. This restraining order is just a piece of paper and means nothing to a monster like him. What you need are self-defense classes and a gun. He will eventually tire of her and come for you, they always do."

Beauty had nodded numbly at the stern woman dressed in a navy suit. Her words echoed through Beauty's mind as she and Knight made their way out of the courtroom. They were in the car headed home when she finally spoke.

"Did you hear what the DA said to me?"

Knight nodded a response, never taking his eyes from the road. Beauty noted the grim set to his lips.

"Do you think she's right?"

Knight nodded again, and Beauty felt that old fear creep up her spine.

"What do I do?" her voice trembled a bit.

This prompted Knight to grasp her hand and reassure her.

"You do nothing. I do something. We got this. My girls will be safe."

It was Beauty's turn to nod and stare at the road.

Knight stayed true to his word. He protected his girls with high-tech security systems and other methods of safety. The King, Queen, and Prince helped as well, finally able to offer Beauty the support system she had been missing for years. They even moved right next door to Knight's house, so they could be close. Everything should have been looking better, and it was... for a while. Then, the Beast did exactly what the DA said he would do.

Beauty lived ninety miles away and he still found ways to get at her. The stalking started with texts, and emails. Then, it was photos of her in her everyday life. Unknown calls. Messages from fake numbers. Little ways for the Beast to let her know he could still get to her.

Beauty tried filing police reports, but they were futile attempts for help. The police told Beauty that he could do all his stalking from burner phones and floating IP addresses, which meant that without a way to trace it back to him, no charges could be filed until he tried to physically harm her or did. The Beast was teaching a new lesson to Beauty. Just because you got away doesn't mean your freedom will come without a price.

This knowledge had Beauty living in constant anxiety. She became reclusive and never went anywhere without a male family member. Days turned to months and Beauty found herself in a fortress of her own making. Still imprisoned because of the Beast, but not his captive. Something happened with the passage of time. The more Beauty had to deal with what had been done to her, the deeper she sank into a darkness she didn't know if she could recover from. She had to live with the fact that her abuser, rapist, captor, boogeyman, was free to live his life and stalk her at will. These facts ate away at her sanity.

It did not help that she was also dealing with a divorce and custody battle at the same time. The Beast was doing his best to prolong and make that situation as hard as possible.

During this time, Beauty got psychological help for herself and the Princess. The Princess responded well to the help and flourished with the support of Beauty and Knight. He gave them exactly what they needed when it came to the kind of love and support that would best benefit their healing. Beauty had a long road ahead of her, but she could finally see the light at the end of her darkness.

The day came for the divorce to be finalized and Beauty was nervous because she would have to see the Beast. With Knight by her side, she stood with her head held high. The Beast got nothing. Not any kind of custody. It turned out, their state did not allow people with family violence convictions to have any kind of custody. The Princess would never have to see him again.

It had taken almost a full year to get the divorce final, but when Beauty walked out of that courtroom with her hand in Knight's, she felt like a weight she had been carrying around for years had been lifted from her shoulders. Even though she felt cold blue eyes on her, Beauty stopped and smiled at the man she loved. He smiled back and gave her a brief kiss on the lips.

Beauty knew the Beast was watching the whole exchange and waiting to throw her a smirk or terrifying look, but she forced herself to not turn around. She walked away with her head held high and never looked back.

EPILOGUE

Happily Ever After...

Exactly one year to the day that she escaped the Beast, Beauty found herself standing in her grandparent's church. It was a beautiful old structure with white columns and gleaming hardwood pews. She wished her grandparents were still alive, as she remembered the day her grandmother had her baptized in this very church. It still looked exactly the same.

Beauty was brought out of her memories at the sound of her little girl's voice.

"How do I look, Mommy?"

Beauty looked down at the gorgeous little

girl in her "fancy" dress and smiled.

"You are the most beautiful girl in the world! How do I look?" The Princess giggled as Beauty smoothed the ivory lace of her simple dress.

"You are the most beautiful, Mommy."

Beauty shook her head from side to side and crouched down to touch her nose to the Princess's.

"Nope. You are. But we can agree to disagree."

With more giggles, the Princess held her little hand out to Beauty's. They clasped hands as the music started and the King took Beauty's arm. The Princess looked nervous and excited as the Prince took her arm.

Beauty whispered to her father. "I love you, Daddy. Happy Birthday."

With pure love shinning in his eyes, he looked at Beauty and smiled.

"This is the best present you could have ever given me. My little girl finally marrying a man who deserves her."

Beauty kissed her father on the cheek and tried to hold back tears as she looked down at the Princess.

"You ready to do this, little darlin?"

With a nod and smile to her brother, the four walked down the aisle where a handsome Knight stood waiting with eyes only for his girls. Beauty smiled at her gorgeous mother as they walked past. Her mother's smile was warm, genuine, and full of love. Beauty never took her eyes off Knight as they approached. A huge grin stretched wide across his face and his eyes glistening with tears.

As the ceremony commenced, the King gave Beauty's hand to Knight. Then, the Prince gave him the Princess's hand.

On that day, in a small church with a simple ceremony with purple flowers, three pieces of one heart were joined together. Surrounded by the people who loved them most.

Finally, after a long journey, Mr. Knight promised to love, cherish, and protect both Beauty and the Princess for as long as he lived.

~ *The End* ~

ABOUT THE AUTHOR

E.L. DuBois was born and raised in Texas where she still lives today surrounded by her amazing family and menagerie of fur babies. She loves to travel, has seen many beautiful places and cannot wait to see more.

Erica's personal experiences with domestic violence has made her an advocate and supporter of great causes facing victims of any harassment or abuse. It is her greatest wish that no one ever has to suffer the traumas she endured, and that justice be brought for all those who have.

She is an avid artist and reader.

In the end Beauty and the Princess found their Knight in Shining Armor. They now live happy, healthy lives with the support of this wonderful man.

Visit E.L. Dubois' Website
www.eldubois.com

CONNECT WITH ERICA:

https://twitter.com/elduboisauthor
https://www.facebook.com/erica.matysiakdubois

88912764R00216

Made in the USA
Middletown, DE
12 September 2018